Julie and Me: Treble Trouble

Alan Gibbons

A Dolphin
Paperback

First published in Great Britain in 2002
as a Dolphin paperback
by Orion Children's Books
a division of the Orion Publishing Group Ltd
Orion House
5 Upper St Martin's Lane
London WC2H 9EA

A catalogue record for this book is available
from the British Library.

Typeset at The Spartan Press Ltd,
Lymington, Hants

Printed in Great Britain by
The Guernsey Press Co Ltd, Guernsey, C.I.

ISBN 1 84255 077 2

For Everton Park Gymnastics Club

PART ONE

Giving the Girl the Cold Shoulder
or
All Over bar the Shouting?

1

Saturday 23rd December
3.10 p.m.

There are two loves in my life: Julie Carter and Manchester United F.C. The Reds are no problem. They've returned every ounce of love I've given them, and more. With every flowing, pulsating attack, with every telling pass and every goal, they tell me I matter. I'm part of the Red Tribe; a winner. It's different with Julie. With every flick of her glossy, black mane of hair, every sulky glance from those deep brown eyes, she cuts me to the quick, tells me I'm nothing. She's going out with somebody else – total pond-life – and it's just breaking my heart.

'Any score, Terry?' shouts Mum.

She isn't really bothered about football; it's more a matter of moral support. She knows what I'll be like if we lose.

'Still 0–0,' I tell her.

I'm pacing the kitchen floor, listening to United – Ipswich on the radio. After three thousand, two hundred and forty minutes of football, two hundred and ninety-six fouls, twenty-eight bookings and one hundred and thirty-three goals, we finally lost our two-year unbeaten home record to Liverpool last week. It's vital we bounce back with a win today.

'Amy and I are nipping down to the shops,' says Mum, sticking her head round the door. 'I don't think we've got enough milk for the holiday.'

'OK.'

That's all there is of the Payne household at the moment: me, Amy and Mum. My dad walked out last summer, saying he 'didn't get the butterflies any more'. He seems to have got them back all of a sudden just lately, though. He goes soppy every time I mention Mum's name. He makes out he's fallen in

3

love with her all over again and he wants to come home, but – and here's the thunderbolt – Mum doesn't want to know. He's made his bed, she reckons, so he can lie in it – on his own.

The change of heart came as quite a surprise. For months it's been Mum who's been the needy one, wanting him back, wishing he'd reconsider. But in the last few weeks she's had a change of heart. I've noticed something different about her, as if she's taken a long, hard look at herself in the mirror and decided to take hold of her life. Good for her, scary for Dad.

The doorbell goes. It's my best mate, Bobby Quinn.

'Room for a little one?' he asks, with the usual twinkle in his eye.

'I thought you'd be out with Emma,' I grunt.

Emma Holland, that is, his latest girlfriend.

'She's in Liverpool, shopping with her mum and sister. What's the score at Old Trafford?'

'0–0.'

'Everton?'

That's Bobby's team. He's a bit of a masochist, my mate.

'Losing 1–0.'

He doesn't look surprised. Well, who would?

'Liverpool did you a favour this morning, didn't they, Terry?'

Not half. After beating us last week at Old Trafford, and very nearly cutting my soul to ribbons, they've just hammered our closest rivals Arsenal 4–0 at Anfield. Weird thing, football. Your worst enemies can become allies overnight. Nothing is ever black and white. A bit like life, really.

'Doing anything over Christmas?' asks Bobby.

'No, family stuff, that's all. You?'

'A couple of parties. I'm taking Emma. That's what I called round for, to see if you wanted to come. The first one's tonight.'

'What, and play gooseberry to you two? No thanks.'

'You can't just sit at home moping over Julie. You know your trouble? You think the sun shines out of her. You've put her on a pedestal.'

Put her there? She climbed up all by herself.

'She's a girl, Terry, not an angel, not a vision, a flesh-and-blood girl. There's plenty more just like her.'

4

Like Julie? No, Bobby, not for me.

'Get back out in the field. I did.'

Didn't he just! For weeks he was dating two girls at once. No sooner had they rumbled him and given him the elbow than he was copping off with Emma. Mr Rebound, that's Bobby, an elastic-band Romeo. He doesn't understand me at all. It's all a game to him. He doesn't see how you can set your heart on just one girl. He's never fallen for anyone the way I've fallen for Julie. Love at first sight means different things to different people. For me it means wanting Julie until it hurts. For Bobby it means loving himself.

'Forget it, Bobby,' I tell him. 'I'm not interested.'

The roar of the crowd alerts me to a goal-scoring opportunity. 1–0. Ole . . . Gunner . . . Solskjaer. I dance round the kitchen, arms raised. The Reds . . . returning the love. I wish Julie was. But she's with Fitz, John Fitzpatrick, the most popular kid in Year 11, captain of the football team and all-round hunk. I think of him, a kind of cross between Brad Pitt and Michael Owen, and then me, a mini Chris Evans and I know I've got no chance with Julie. She's out of my league.

Solskjaer's through again. 2–0. He is my Solskjaer, my Ole Solskjaer.

'We're back,' I crow. 'We're back.'

I'm back too. Last week, I was dead and buried. I'd lost my girl and we'd lost to the arch-enemy, Liverpool. Can there be a worse place to be a Man U. fan than here in Prescot on the eastern rim of Merseyside?

There are ten Scousers for every Manc round here, and every one of them's been asking me the score. I was gutted, humiliated. Now, just a few days later, I can hold my head up, and it's all down to the Reds, returning the love.

'Sure you're not coming tonight? Emma's got a couple of mates . . .'

I wrinkle my nose.

'Nah, don't feel like it.'

'It's your funeral. I'll give you a ring tomorrow.'

'Yes, see you Bobby.'

He bumps into Mum and Amy at the front door. I hear them talking.

'Why don't you go to that party?' asks Mum, emptying the shopping bags. 'It'll do you good.'

'I don't want to, OK?'

Mum holds her hands up.

'Only asking. I still don't know why you had to finish with Chloe. She's such a lovely girl.'

Chloe Blackburn, my first girlfriend. In fact, the only one so far. Yes, she is a lovely girl. But she wasn't Julie.

'You know why,' I retort. 'I like somebody else.'

'Who?'

'Julie Carter.'

'You're a silly lad,' says Mum. 'It's obvious this Julie's not interested.'

But that's the thing, Mum, she *is* interested. I can't quite believe it, but she's got feelings for me too. She told me so only last week. What did she say? *Why didn't you tell me four months ago?* Before she went out with Fitz, that is.

I had hope for us then, real hope. Then something happened, a stupid misunderstanding. And now she's back with Fitz, lousy, smirking Fitz. Plastic Scouser Fitz.

'Mum, it's my life.'

That's right, it's my life, and I'll cock it up my own way.

Tuesday 26th December
12.40 p.m.

If that's Christmas, you can keep it.

It was the tale of two turkeys, three if you count my dad. I had Christmas dinner with Mum and Amy and Gran and Grandad Thompson. The turkey was moist, the sprouts were firm and my thoughts were elsewhere . . . with Julie, where else?

Is she with Fitz? Is she happy?

I had Christmas tea with Dad and Amy in his scabby flat. The turkey was burnt and the sprouts had dissolved into a green mush, so we had TV dinners on our knees and I was still thinking about Julie.

Do they have mistletoe? Are they kissing?

That was Christmas Day. It came, it went, it was rubbish. Still, at least life's half-way back to normal now. There's a full

6

football programme today. Arsenal have already kicked off. They're 1–0 up against Leicester through Henry. I suck in my breath. If they run out winners, we've got to beat Villa away to keep our eight-point lead at the top.

'Oh, it's not football again,' moans Amy, walking into the living room.

My little sister doesn't understand The Beautiful Game.

'I'm afraid so.'

'I wish you and Dad still went to the match,' she says.

You and me both, Amy. My season ticket was a victim of Mum and Dad's separation. Family finances just don't run to it any more. I have to make do with Sky Sports instead. The Villa-United game starts with relentless United pressure.

Giggs, Solskjaer and Butt all have good chances. After twenty minutes we've had sixty per cent of possession, but it's still 0–0.

Zero progress, like Julie and me.

At Highbury Arsenal are running away with it. They're 3–1 up. At Villa Park, Paul Scholes goes close with a header. Another newsflash from Highbury. Now it's 4–1. The pressure is on us to come up with a goal. We reach half-time. United's possession stands at seventy per cent, astonishing for the away team, but no breakthrough.

Same as Julie and me.

Meanwhile, the news from Highbury has got even worse. Arsenal have battered Leicester 6–1. I'm on the edge of my seat, willing the Reds to score, but as the minutes go by I'm becoming more and more tense. All that possession and nothing to show for it. Beckham's crosses don't have the usual zip, Ole Solskjaer's killer instinct seems to have deserted him.

'Come on, lads.'

Six minutes to go and I'm losing hope.

Then the breakthrough comes. Beckham crosses, Solskjaer scores with a sweet header. How could I have doubted them?

Villa 0, United 1.

We've broken their unbeaten home record and hung onto our eight-point lead. Suddenly, it dawns on me, there's a lesson in this, Terry lad. United haven't had it all easy this season. We got turned over by Chelsea in the Charity Shield.

We lost to Arsenal and Liverpool, but did we fold? Did we heck! We had that bit of steel. Keep your nerve, hold on to what you know to be true, and things are bound to turn out all right in the end. Keep your nerve, that's it! I've done enough chasing round after Julie. Who wants somebody who acts all forlorn and desperate?

I'm not going to be a little, lovesick puppy any more, trailing round after her, embarrassing myself. The lovelorn bit hasn't worked, so I've got to change tack. I'm going to salvage some dignity. I'll take a leaf out of United's book. What I need is tactics, a strategy. I'm going to play it cool. Wouldn't that be a novelty? No matter how often she glances round, she won't catch me looking at her soulfully. No matter how much I'm tempted, I'll be looking the other way.

Thursday 28th December
8.30 a.m.

I'm woken by Amy squealing her head off. Her best friend Katie slept over last night and she's squealing too.

'Mum, Terry, come and look. It snowed in the night.'

I stagger to the window in my boxer shorts. Amy's right. It's a total white-out. Everywhere's covered in a blanket of snow, two or three inches at least. I watch for a few moments then climb back into bed. My mind starts playing a game of What Ifs.

What if you could win the Double or win Julie? Which would you choose?

What if you could get Mum and Dad back together or win Julie? What then?

I shake my head. Even if life was like that, how could I choose?

But what if life turned out the way it ought to? Me and Julie together, United winning the Premiership and the Champions' League, Dad back where he belongs, that would be my idea of heaven on earth. The trill of my mobile breaks in on my thoughts.

'Hello?'

'You up yet, misery guts?'

It's Bobby. I didn't think he knew half past eight existed!

'Get up, you lazy dog.'

This is Bobby calling me lazy! We're talking pots, kettles and the colour black.

'I'm calling for Emma on my way to yours,' he says. 'You're going to enjoy yourself, and that's an order. Snowtime!'

'But . . .'

It's too late to tell him I'd rather stay in and feel sorry for myself. He's already hung up.

'Terry love,' Mum calls, 'Would you take Amy and Katie to the park? They're really excited.'

'But I was going out with Bobby.'

'Where?'

'Snowball fight.'

'Perfect. You can take the girls with you.'

Her voice changes. She's obviously talking to Amy and Katie.

'Terry will take you to the park.'

The announcement is met with deafening cheers.

Thursday 28th December
10.00 a.m.

'I know,' shouts Bobby. 'Snow angels.'

He throws himself on his back, flapping his arms to make wings in the snow. Before I know it, Emma, Amy and Katie have joined him, laughing like mad things.

'Come in and join us, Terry. The snow's lovely.'

Oh well, in for a penny, in for a pound. I flop down, flapping my arms.

I take my eyes off the others just long enough for them to pound me with snowballs.

'Right,' I declare, clawing up handfuls of snow. 'You're dead.'

Within moments I'm in the thick of a furious snowball fight. My ears and cheeks are burning with the cold and slowly melting snow is running down my back, but I couldn't care less. I'm having fun.

'Who wants to help me build a snowman?' asks Emma.

Amy and Katie are jumping up and down, shouting: 'Me, me!'

'She's good with them,' I say, watching Emma organising the girls.

'Yes, she's great,' says Bobby approvingly.

'Are you going to do the right thing by this one?' I ask.

'Meaning?'

I'm thinking about his exe's, Caitlin and Rosie.

'No two-timing her.'

Bobby winks.

'You never know, Terry lad, you never know.'

He jogs over to help with the snowman. I shake my head. The sun's come out and it's gleaming on the spire of Prescot parish church in the distance. It's a picture postcard scene. A gang of lads are playing football. My thoughts go back three weeks to footy practice. At a quarter to four that Wednesday afternoon Julie had all but told me she was going to dump Fitz. By half past my hopes were dashed. And all because of a stupid misunderstanding. I close my eyes and I'm there on the pitch. Fitz is goading me: *You'll never take my place in this team. You are the weakest link.* We go for a fifty-fifty ball. He's got his studs up. *You are the weakest link, goodbye.* I refuse to pull out. I will not back down. There's a sickening crunch, then a loud scream. It's Fitz. I've broken his ankle.

It was an accident, Julie, an accident.

But she'll never believe that now. And that's why she's with him, because he's a victim, and I'm a thug.

But it wasn't like that, Julie. It wasn't like that at all.

'Hey Terry,' shouts Bobby. 'Get over here. You don't think you're leaving all the hard work to us, do you?'

I smile and join in. As if by magic, Bobby has produced a carrot for the snowman's nose and a couple of two-pence pieces for the eyes when I hear familiar voices. Kelly Magee and Gary Tudor, Fitz and . . . Julie. The four of them are pretty much inseparable.

Gary's the first to say anything: 'Well, if it isn't Chopper Payne.'

I scowl.

'It was an accident, Gary.'

'Yes, sure it was. You're such a little innocent, just like Roy Keane.'

Fitz lets his mate do the talking. He stands propped up on his

10

crutches, enjoying my discomfort. He's clever like that. He knows the best way to Julie's heart is to play the victim. And, boy, doesn't he milk it! Look at him, all blue eyes and Michael Owen haircut; you'd think butter wouldn't melt in his mouth. I can feel Julie's eyes on me, but I refuse to meet them, even though it's killing me. These new tactics, I never thought they'd be so tough to put into action.

As they turn to go, Fitz stumbles. Julie puts an arm round his waist to support him.

'He did that on purpose,' says Bobby. 'For your benefit.'

'Tell me something I don't know,' I say.

'Move on,' says Bobby. 'You're flogging a dead horse.'

I watch Julie and Fitz crossing the park. Now that she's got her back to me, it's safe to look. Flogging a dead horse? Maybe. All these months and I'm no closer to taking her out.

But I can still remember her words before the practice match when it all went wrong: *If only you'd told me four months ago*. And she kissed me. I'm not imagining it. It happened. I can still feel the press of her lips on mine. That sort of feeling doesn't just vanish because of a misunderstanding.

There's something there. I know there is. Fitz isn't right for you, Julie. You're not happy with him. If only I could talk to you alone, just for a few minutes, if only I could explain. But I won't plead and I won't beg. I'm not going to run after you, Julie Carter. I've got my pride. No matter how hard it is, every time I see you I'm not going to give myself away.

Sunday 31st December
10.30 p.m.

I knew this was a mistake. I knew it the moment Bobby persuaded me into it. Going to a New Year's party in my frame of mind. Am I mad? For starters, the moment we arrived Bobby left me on my own to dance with Emma. Then my ex, Chloe, showed up with Jamie Sneddon. Every time I turn round, she's there with him. I think she's trying to tell me what I'm missing. As if I haven't suffered enough, Fitz has just arrived with Julie. I might have guessed they'd be here. I'm sticking to my promise, though. Every time I come near Julie I'm Mr Cool, at least on the outside. I said I wouldn't go trailing after her, and I'm not. So here I am sitting on my own in a corner watching everybody else either dancing or copping off. Whoever said you never feel so lonely as when you're in the middle of a crowd got it dead right. I become aware of somebody talking to me:

'You haven't seen Bobby, have you Terry?'

It's Emma.

'No, I thought he was with you.'

'He was. I got talking to one of my mates and he just disappeared.'

Oh oh, no Bobby, you wouldn't.

'I've been all round the house looking for him.'

Not right under her nose. Bobby, you wouldn't.

'He's probably just in the loo.'

Emma smiles thinly. I think she's got an inkling.

'Yes, maybe.'

That's when I hear pandemonium in the kitchen.

Please, not Bobby.

A voice rasps over the beat of the CD player:

'I'll have you, Quinn. Outside, now!'

It's Paul Scully. He's lashing out at somebody, or at least trying to. Gary Tudor's pulling him back. That's when I see Bobby. He's got a red mark above his eye, and he's looking a bit embarrassed. Paul's still trying to get at him.

'Snogging my bird, the dirty little get.'

I catch sight of Pepsey Cooper, Paul's girlfriend. She looks upset, you know, caught-at-it upset. Her mascara's running. Bobby, you idiot. Right under Emma's nose, and Paul's. Talk about asking for it. Paul gets a hand free and thumps Bobby smack on the nose. It takes Gary and a couple of other lads to restrain him. I glance round at Emma. Her eyes are welling up. Oh great! Now I'm going to have to take care of her. She turns and heads for the door.

'Emma!'

I glare at Bobby. This was bound to happen some time. I'm about to follow Emma when I come face to face with Julie. Am I mistaken, or is she following me round? I'm tempted to speak to her. My God, are the tactics working? Great, here's Julie pursuing *me* and I've got my hands full with Emma. Aaargh!

'Emma, you can't go home alone, not when you're upset.'

Even as I'm saying it, I'm actually hoping she can. She looks at me.

'How could he do that to me, Terry? How?'

I notice Julie standing on the doorstep, watching us. What do I do? I just want to dump Emma and run to Julie. But Emma's suffering. Bobby's done the dirty on her and she needs a friend. That's what I'm good at, being a friend. This is killing me, Julie, just killing me. I take Emma's arm and lead her away.

'Come on, Emma, I'll walk you home.'

What am I, some sort of rotten saint?

Emma smiles.

'You're a nice guy, Terry.'

Yes, that's me, nice guy, but you know what they say about nice guys? They never get the girl. Emma kisses me on the cheek. My face starts to burn. What if Julie saw us? What if she takes it the wrong way? As Emma and I walk off down the street, I'm dying to know if Julie's still watching. Did she want to talk to me? And what about? But I don't look back. I'm not going to chase after her like a lovesick kid. I'm doing the right thing. I know I am.

Aren't I?

Monday 1st January 2001
One minute past midnight

I'm on my own again. I have been since eleven o'clock. Emma and I were just turning into her street when Bobby came panting up. It was all a mistake, he said, a misunderstanding. Just let me explain. And Emma let him. That's how I left them, with Bobby in grovel mode and Emma slowly thawing. He'll win her round. That's what he does, Bobby. He charms people.

Since then I've been wandering round, killing time. I must have relived every moment of my pursuit of Julie, the first sight of her in the school gym, the time she got together with Fitz at the school disco, the time she kissed me. I told Mum I'd be home by half past midnight. See in the New Year and come straight home. So I wasn't about to turn up an hour and a half early. I don't want her thinking I'm a loser.

Which I suppose I am. Especially if Julie thought Emma and

I . . . It's nagging at me. Not another misunderstanding. I mean, that's two to explain, and I'm no Bobby. I don't do charm. It's a relief to see the fireworks and hear the strains of Auld Lang Syne. Now I can head home and put a brave face on a disastrous evening. I turn into our street and groan.

It's Dad. He's rotten drunk and he's shouting his head off:

'Just give me another chance, Sharon. I love you.'

Except it comes out *Ahlurrvya*.

He says it over and over again:

Ahlurrvya, ahlurrvya, ahlurrvya.

Then he sinks to his knees on the pavement.

Oh Dad!

All the neighbours are looking. Mum's at the window too.

'Terry, would you get him out of here?'

'Dad, get up,' I plead. 'I'll take you home.'

'But I love her,' he says.

It comes out *Ahlurrverr*.

Ahlurrverr, ahrlurrverr, ahlurrverr.

'I know you do, Dad,' I say, guiding him in the direction of his flat. 'But this isn't the way to show it.'

'Then what is, Terry?'

As we stagger away I lift my eyes to the sky. I remember Emma kissing me on the cheek. Then I think of the way I ignored Julie. It seemed a good idea at the time. Now I'm not so sure.

'Tell me, Terry, what is the way to show it?'

I have to give him an honest reply.

'I don't know, Dad. I just don't know.'

2

Strategy, I call it. Keeping my dignity, I call it. Hah? Suicide is more like it. What was I thinking of? The very idea of me, the skinny ginger nut with the number one skinhead crop, the many-freckled failure, Mr Won't Get Any GCSEs, the poor man's Chris Evans deciding to ignore somebody as drop-dead gorgeous as Julie Carter. As if she's even noticed! She's too busy with her Michael Owen lookalike boyfriend and her Sabrina lookalike best mate Kelly. What is it with Julie? Why does she have to collect stereotypes? What next? A Lassie dog? A Royle Family mum and dad? Of course, I could be her Chris Evans nerd stereotype, though that hardly bears thinking about. It's been the best part of a month I've been ignoring her, and, in all that time – every single one of the twenty-eight days I've kept up my *strategy* – I'll bet she hasn't given me a second thought. All I've done is leave the way wide open for Fitz. Some competition I am. Just when the strains in their relationship are starting to show I start pretending she doesn't exist. Nice one, Terry! As I head over to Dad's flat to watch the FA Cup fourth-round tie against West Ham, I try to get my head straight. What on earth do I do now? She hasn't even spoken to me in a month, never mind decided to dump Fitz for me. My mobile goes. For a crazy split second I fantasise that it might be Julie on the other end of the line. It isn't. It's Bobby.

'Where are you?'

'Here.'

I hear his sucked-in breath.

'And where's here?'

'I'm on my way to my dad's, to watch the match.'

'Well, du-uh.'

'Do you want to come over and watch it?'

'Forget it. Did you know that people in the UK spend an average two hundred and fifteen minutes a day watching TV?'

I didn't.

'Anyway,' says Bobby. 'I've sworn off football. Bad for my health.'

That's on account of Everton getting battered 3–0 at home by First Division Tranmere Rovers. Bobby just can't take the humiliation. Or the heart palpitations.

'Do you want to do something later?' he asks.

'Sure. Where's Emma?'

'She's sleeping over at a friend's house. Girl thing.'

So he obviously needs me for a boy thing.

'Call in at mine about five. I'll be back by then.'

'And through to the fifth round of the Cup,' says Bobby. 'You'll murder West Ham.'

I hope he's right. Somehow, I'm pretty relaxed about it. We beat them 3–1 in the league just twenty-seven days ago, and should have scored more. They were as limp as week-old lettuce. We could have got into double figures.

'See you later, then.'

'Yes, see you Terry.'

As I jog up the stairs to Dad's flat I can hear the strains of 'Don't Let the Sun Catch You Crying' by Gerry and the Pacemakers. It must be centuries old, from the Record Collection that Time Forgot. When is Dad going to pull himself together? I find the door open. For a moment, I feel quite spooked. I'm thinking Marie Celeste.

'You there, Dad?'

'Yes, come in Terry.'

Phew, he hasn't slipped into a parallel universe or anything like that.

I look around for a place to sit. Dad seems to have forgotten his resolution not to have a guy-flat. When he first moved in, he used to keep it neat but suddenly there are microwave meal trays and drinks cans on the coffee table, there's a pair of undies on the CD player and the carpet doesn't look like it's been vacuumed in weeks. He's obviously stuck in yearning mode. Message to brain: don't mention Mum in front of him.

'I thought you'd have the match coverage on,' I say.

'It's ITV,' says Dad. 'Who wants to listen to Terry Venables rabbitting on?'

Funny, Dad's always rated El Tel, even if he is a Cockney. I decide his behaviour has got more to do with male auto-destruct than his real verdict on TV football pundits, and let it pass without comment.

'So can I put it on now?'

'Go ahead, I need a win to cheer me up.'

Just lately, Dad whines louder than a pair of Boeing 747 engines. And he's got less lift.

Be patient, I tell myself. It's a phase he's got to get through.

Sunday 28th January
4 p.m.

Some phase! Suddenly Dad's going into overdrive.

His job's rubbish, his flat's rubbish, now his team's rubbish. Only he doesn't say rubbish – somebody pass the swear box.

His self-pitying whine reaches a crescendo in the seventy-sixth minute of the match. This is how he descends into emotional meltdown:

Paolo Di Canio beats United's offside trap as Kanoute's pass dissects our defence.

Moaning reaches 7 on the Richter scale.

The United defenders stand appealing for offside.

7.2 on the Richter scale.

The linesman's flag stays down.

7.8.

Barthez in the United goal continues to appeal. He looks like a schoolboy asking for the loo.

8.0.

Di Canio puts the ball in the net. Now Barthez looks like a schoolboy who's forgotten his homework.

That's a big 9.5 on the Richter scale. Any minute now he'll go off the scale altogether.

'Rubbish, absolute rubbish,' is Dad's verdict.

Boing!

When I dare to contradict him, pointing out that we outplayed the Hammers in the first half, that we're thirteen

17

points clear at the top of the Premiership and well-placed in the Champions' League, not only does he not stop whining, he actually accuses me of **not caring**! What's he on about? Even when I was at nursery school I cared. One Monday morning the teacher asked each of us to sing our favourite rhyme. You know what I chose? Glory, glory Man United!

'Me!' I retort angrily. '*Me*, not care? Who cancelled our season tickets, Dad? Go on, who put his gym subscription before the Reds? We could have been there today at the Theatre of Dreams. But you wanted to get fit, just so you could cop off with Mule.'

Dad doesn't like being reminded about Muriel. The memory of him going out with a size 12 perma-tanned gym bunny is the biggest obstacle to Mum taking him back. What woman likes being dumped for a younger, slimmer model?

'Oh, rub salt in the wounds, why don't you?' he snaps.

'Dad, the only wounds you've got are entirely self-inflicted. What did you expect? That Mum would take you back with open arms the moment you got fed up of your . . .'

The word *floozy* pops into my head. It's a word Mum might use, but it would sound ridiculous coming from me.

'My what?'

'Your . . . your . . . MULE!'

We stand glaring at each other, veins bulging, eyeballs popping.

An imaginary exchange goes through my mind. It ends with Dad calling me an ungrateful pup and me calling him a loser. Luckily, we both keep our mouths shut.

'I'm going,' I say.

'Fine,' he says.

'Fine.'

'Fine.'

'Bye.'

'Yes, bye.'

Sunday 28th January
5.15 p.m.

'Do you want to know the Cup draw?' asks Mum.

'No,' I say.

'No way,' says Bobby.

Who cares? Our teams are both out of the competition. Amy giggles. Bobby and I give her daggers, as if reminding her that little sisters can be easily kebabed.

'Another bacon butty?' asks Mum.

She's obviously trying to console us after the soccer catastrophes of the weekend. What becomes of the broken-hearted? I'll tell you: they gross out on rashers of prime back bacon.

'Wouldn't mind,' says Bobby.

Does he ever? The boy's got the digestive system of a great white shark. One of these days he'll cough up a car number-plate.

'Anyway,' says Bobby, 'what's that you're eating, Mrs P?'

'She's on Carol Vorderman's detox diet,' Amy informs him.

'Oh,' says Bobby. 'Stale buns and rabbit food. My old lady had a go at that.'

'Did she lose weight?' asks Mum hopefully.

'Nah, just friends. It was all those sprouts. Gave her gas.'

Mum frowns. I'm not sure whether it's because of the mention of gas or because the diet hasn't got a hundred per cent approval rating. She's desperate for a quick fix.

'I think that must be a different diet,' she says.

'Talking of gas,' says Bobby. 'Did you know that, on average, people break wind fifteen times a day?'

'Yes,' says Mum, wrinkling her nose. 'I saw the advert on telly. And before you say anything, I still think men are a lot worse than women.'

'Not according to the statistics,' says Bobby.

My best mate is a real facts and figures nerd.

'Bobby,' says Mum, 'I'll bet you it's men who come up with those statistics.'

'Could be,' says Bobby. 'It's a man's world.'

'Mm,' says Mum, 'that's half the problem. In fact, it's the whole problem.'

I grimace. For him, maybe. He's had more girlfriends than most kids have had zits. But the world doesn't belong to this particular guy. I take after Dad, a loser in love.

'Anyway,' says Mum, 'seeing as you lads are going to inherit the Earth, you won't mind doing the washing-up. I've got a phone call to make.'

She's about to go when she turns round.

'Would you baby-sit for me on Wednesday, Terry?'

'No problem,' I say. 'We're playing Sunderland away. I'll be listening to the match on the radio anyway. So what're you doing?'

There's a brief pause.

'You are joking!' she says, walking out.

I stand in a puddle of bewilderment. Now what have I done?

'Parents' evening, you dope,' says Bobby.

Fancy forgetting that. It's like a turkey getting amnesia about Christmas.

'Got any biccies?' Bobby asks.

'None in the house,' I say. 'Mum doesn't want any temptation, so we're all on a diet.'

Amy nods ruefully.

'That's right. There isn't even ice-cream.'

'So what do you have for afters?'

'Fruit or yoghurt.'

Bobby looks unimpressed.

'We'll go down the offie later,' he says. 'Stock up on illicit chocolate.'

All of a sudden I know what Al Capone got out of Prohibition.

'Will you get me something?' asks Amy, brightening.

'Sure,' says Bobby. 'Raid the piggy bank.'

'I've got a steel cash box,' says Amy stuffily. 'To stop him getting in.'

By *him* she means *me*. I act all offended.

'When did I ever raid your money box?'

'Four years ago when you wanted that Man U. annual.'

'Oh yes, I forgot. Sorry.'

We wash up then head down to the offie.

'So how's it going with Emma?' I ask. 'Has she stopped bringing up the Pepsey Cooper incident yet?'

'Just about,' says Bobby.

There's a twinkle in his eye as he adds:

'It was worth it though. She's got lips like a limpet, that Pepsey. Snogs the gob off you.'

'Bobby, you're disgusting.'

'What, just because you're not getting anywhere?'

That's a low blow.

'How long is it since you last talked to the lovely Julie?'

'You know very well. It was New Year's Eve.'

'Still ignoring her?' he asks mischievously.

'OK,' I admit. 'So it was a dumb idea. What do you suggest?'

'I suggest,' says Bobby nice and slow so it sinks in, 'that you forget all about her.'

Monday 29th January
12.45 p.m.

I'm sitting on one of the new benches near the Sports Hall. They're meant to be for anyone who wants to read or sit quietly. Of course, the moment Fitz lays eyes on me, he has a different interpretation.

'Found the Billy-No-Mates seats, have you?' he sneers.

Gary Tudor and Paul Scully laugh appreciatively, egging him on to have another dig.

'Did you enjoy the match?' he asks. 'I know I did.'

I knew this was coming. Kicked out of the FA Cup in the early stages. I feel so humiliated.

'Get stuffed.'

'Funny,' says Fitz, 'I thought that's what happened to United.'

'Did you see Barthez standing with his arm up?' chuckles Paul. 'What a divvy.'

'Please, Mr Di Canio,' says Gary in a really stupid, whining voice, 'don't kick the ball past me.'

He's trying to sound French, but it's more Welsh than anything.

'You can't be onside. You're playing Man U.'

The next minute, the three of them are standing with their hands up.

'Go on,' I grumble. 'Have your fun.'

'Oh, I intend to,' says Fitz. 'Especially now the plaster cast's off.'

I wince at the memory of my mistimed tackle, not because it hurt Fitz, he was asking for it, but because it pushed Julie back into his arms. Fancy feeling sorry for that moron. I wish I'd broken his neck as well.

'I'll be playing again in a month to six weeks,' he says. 'Then I'm taking my place back.'

I thought that would be getting to him. I did well in training last week and Six Guns is going to give me a start in the team in our next match. It's great, I'm replacing Fitz.

I intend to make the most of it. What wouldn't I give to put one over on Frisky Fitzy.

'You're going to have to fight for it,' I tell him, managing a cosmetic yawn of contempt.

Fitz's eyes narrow.

'You wait, MnM,' he says.

(That's my new nickname, MnM, short for Mad Manc).

'I'll fight you all right.'

Gary and Paul think Fitz means competition on the pitch, but I know what really happened in our collision.

I know which of us put his studs up first and which of us meant to do damage. No, when he says fight he means it. We're talking GBH. Fair enough, if that's the way he wants to play it.

'Two home defeats in a month,' says Fitz. 'Do you think the wheels are coming off the Man U. bandwagon?'

'You wish,' I say defiantly.

'Aw, diddums lose to ums nasty Cockneys?' taunts Fitz.

It's his parting shot. They move away, laughing and pushing. I stare at my feet.

'Penny for them,' says a voice.

I look up.

'Oh, hi there Emma.'

Emma's smiling. Smiles suit her. I'd forgotten how attractive she is.

'Seen Bobby?'

'No. That's why I'm sitting here. Nothing to do.'

I remember what Fitz said: the Mad Manc in his Billy-No-Mates seat.

'You can talk to me.'

She sits down next to me.

'How did your mocks go?'

My shoulders sag.

'They didn't.'

'That bad, eh?'

'They've put me in a booster class for Maths. Mum will go mad.'

'I don't see why,' said Emma, 'You can't be good at everything.'

'I'm not that good at anything,' I say. 'Me and exams don't mix. It's a bit like sincerity and politicians.'

'Bit like me then,' says Emma cheerfully. 'I've got a brain the size of a pea.'

'I'm sure that's not true.'

'All right,' she says with her heart-stopping smile. 'A broad bean then. Honestly, I'm not very academic.'

It's my turn to smile. When I'm around Paul and Gary, and especially Fitz, I feel really inadequate. They're all in the top set for everything, same as Julie. You know who I am: Billy-No-Brains in his Billy-No-Mates seat.

'I'm Bobby's dream woman,' says Emma. 'Pretty but dim.'

Actually, she's more than *pretty*. If it wasn't for Julie . . . and the fact that she's my best mate's girl . . .

'You're not dim!' I protest.

'Thanks.'

She brushes a loose thread from her skirt. Her knee touches mine. A mild electric shock shudders through me.

'Listen to us,' she says. 'We sound like card-carrying members of the Low Esteem Club. You know what we need, a booster class in self-confidence.'

Personally, I can't see that she's short on self-confidence at all.

'To tell you the truth, Emma,' I say, 'I couldn't take much more boosting. I think I'm all boosted out.'

She laughs. It reminds me of the times I've made Julie laugh. It's nice making a girl laugh. It makes you feel . . . somebody.

'Does Bobby talk about me much?' she asks.

Suddenly I don't feel somebody any more. I'm just somebody's mate.

'All the time,' I fib.

'Liar.'

She can obviously see right through me. What am I supposed to do, tell the girl the truth, that she's his latest *squeeze*, OK to be going on with but nothing serious?

'You don't need to stick up for him, you know,' she says. 'I know exactly what Bobby's like. I haven't forgotten New Year.'

I'm starting to feel uncomfortable. Where's this going? She soon tells me.

'Bobby's a laugh, but we're going nowhere fast. I'm beginning to wonder whether I went out with the wrong friend.'

She gives my hand a squeeze. The mild shock is replaced by seismic Death Row convulsions.

Oh my God, I'm being squeezed by the squeeze! My skin prickles and my throat goes dry. This I didn't expect!

'Emma,' I stammer, 'Bobby's my best mate.'

'Yes, and you're very loyal. I'm not sure if he deserves you. I don't know whether he deserves either of us.'

She has inched closer. I can smell the sweet mixture of perfume and girl-hair. Oh crumbs!

'You were lovely to me at New Year, a real gentleman.'

Gentleman, *me*? I don't feel much of a gentleman right now. I feel hot, bothered, confused, tempted. Emma's looking right into my eyes. I don't know where to put myself.

'I needed a friend that night. Thanks.'

With that, she gives me a peck on the cheek. And, would you believe it, just as her lips touch my skin, Julie walks out of the Sports Hall accompanied by Kelly McGee. Dinner-time gymnastics club. How did I forget?

No-o-o-o!

Julie stares at me like I'm some slavering dog on heat, then jogs towards the library. I can't help stealing a look at her legs. Kelly, self-appointed secretary of the No-to-Mad-Mancs Society, scowls at me then trots after Julie. No doubt she'll soon be sticking the knife into me. Emma Holland, your timing's incredible!

'Oh wonderful,' I groan. 'Just wonderful!'

'Still carrying that torch for Julie Carter, are you?'

Emma sounds disappointed.

'What do you think?'

'I might just have done you a favour,' she says.

'How do you work that out?' I bleat.

'I might just have made her jealous.'

I shake my head. Chance would be a fine thing!

Mum knocks on the bedroom door.

'Can I have your duvet cover for the wash?'

'Hang on.'

I start unbuttoning the cover. Mum pops her head round the door.

'You need to do a tidy up in here.'

'Yes, in a minute. One thing at a time.'

I'm wrestling with the duvet and the duvet's winning. My mobile goes. Mum passes it to me. I read the last two digits. It's Bobby.

'I think I'll let it ring,' I say, finally overcoming the duvet's resistance.

'Have you two fallen out?' Mum asks.

'No, of course not.'

'Then why aren't you answering?'

I go all hot.

'Don't feel like it.'

Mum gives me a sideways look. It suddenly strikes me that her face looks thinner. Would you believe it, her diet is actually working.

'Anything you'd like to tell me?' she asks.

Normally I'd die rather than confide in Mum, but I'm short of shoulders to cry on. Dad's suffering from a terminal case of Self-Pity Syndrome and I can hardly tell Bobby that his girlfriend's got the hots for me, can I? Pathetically, that just about exhausts my list of confidants.

'It's a bit embarrassing.'

'Go on.'

'You know Emma?'

'Bobby's girl Emma?'

'Yes. She kind of came on to me today.'

'Oh dear.'

I thought Mum would be appalled. Since Dad's fling with Mule, she's really down on love-cheats. Not that she ever had much time for them in the first place. Very straight-laced, my mum. But just lately, every time infidelity is mentioned on TV or in the paper, she jumps on her soapbox.

Really bitter.

'Is that it? Oh dear?'

'What did you expect?'

'Dunno. More than *Oh dear*.'

'It happens.'

I snort.

'Not to me, it doesn't.'

'I don't see why not. Don't put yourself down. You're a good-looking lad.'

'Behave.'

'No, you are.'

Come to think of it, Chloe Blackburn liked me, and Julie sort of . . . kind of . . . now Emma, she definitely likes me. That's three really cute girls. Maybe I'm not such a loser, after all.

'So what do I do about it?'

Mum smiles.

'The question is: what *did* you do about it?'

'Nothing. Bobby's my best mate.'

'Then I think you did the right thing.'

I smile.

'Nothing, you mean?'

'Exactly. You didn't let anybody down. Not Bobby, not Emma, not yourself. You were a good friend.'

That again!

'Yes, you're right Mum.'

'It doesn't matter if other people want to behave badly,' she says. 'You've got to be able to look yourself in the mirror.'

I think of Bobby. He behaves badly on a regular basis and he has no trouble looking in the mirror. He loves himself to bits. He could look like the Elephant Man and still put on as many airs as Brad Pitt.

'What are you two talking about?' asks Amy, arriving with her duvet cover.

'I was just saying what a good-looking lad your big brother is,' says Mum.

Amy lets out this paint-stripping shriek of laughter.

'Him!'

Go on, I think, build my self-confidence, why don't you?

'I think you ought to ring Bobby,' says Mum, leaving with the laundry. 'After all, you didn't do anything, did you?'

'You're right, Mum. Thanks.'

I ring Bobby back. While I wait for him to answer I think about what Mum said.

No, I didn't do anything.

I never do.

3

Wednesday 31st January
5.15 p.m.

'Good performance, lads,' says Six Guns, applauding us off the pitch.

We've just won 2–0 against St Thomas Aquinas. I had a good game, clearing off the line when it was still 0–0 and setting up our first for Jamie Sneddon. He didn't thank me for the assist, of course. I still haven't been forgiven for breaking Fitz's ankle. Jamie just ran across to the touchline and waved to Chloe Blackburn, my ex. They started going out the moment I dumped her. The rebound effect. Or is it the *Up yours* effect?

'Good goals, Gary and Jamie,' says Six Guns. 'Busy work in midfield, Terry.'

A couple of pairs of eyes turn in my direction. Any recognition for my efforts is pretty grudging, but it is there. Maybe, just maybe, memories of what happened back in December are beginning to fade. One person who'll never forget is Fitz. He's watched the whole game from the touchline, with Julie by his side. His brooding presence makes sure nobody actually congratulates me.

'I won't be long,' I tell Amy who is standing shivering all by herself in the drizzle.

Mum works until half past five so I have to pick Amy up from school and bring her back here with me so I can play. I feel quite sorry for her, really. It must be boring just standing there, not knowing anyone. I've got to get a move on. It's parents' evening tonight and Mum is going straight to the school after work.

'Hurry up,' says Amy, 'I'm freezing, and it's starting to rain.'

28

When I come out of the changing room, I get a surprise. It's throwing it down. That isn't the surprise. It's done nothing else this year. No, what I didn't expect was to see Amy sheltering under Julie's umbrella.

'She was getting drenched,' says Julie. 'This isn't really fair on her.'

'I know,' I say, 'But Mum is working. No alternative.'

'You could get a baby-sitter,' says Julie. 'Lots of us do it for extra cash.'

Is that some sort of offer? My pulse rate accelerates.

'Thanks for sheltering her,' I mumble, not quite sure what to say next.

'Where's Fitz?' pops out inevitably.

'Talking to Gary and Jamie somewhere.'

There's something in the tone of her voice that gives me hope. She isn't quite the adoring girlfriend.

'Looking forward to tonight?' asks Julie.

'Parents' evening?' I ask. 'No chance.'

Julie will be all right. She's in top set for everything. University material. I've only made it in English and French. The conversation sags between us. Questions hang in the air, but they remain unanswered. Amy stands between me and a meaningful conversation. Fitz appears and waves to Julie. Julie acknowledges him.

'Hang on,' she says as Amy and I turn to go. 'Here.'

She produces a rolled umbrella from her bag.

'It's Kelly's. You can borrow it for tonight.'

'Thanks.'

I stare after Julie, wondering if they mean something, the umbrella and the mention of baby-sitting.

'You like her, don't you?' asks Amy.

'Don't be daft,' I say.

Daft? She's anything but.

Wednesday 31st January
8.05 p.m.

'How long will Mum be?' asks Amy.

She picks her times, my little sister. It's Sunderland (third in the Premiership) against United (first), what they call a six-

29

pointer. Kevin Phillips has just pulled the trigger for the Black Cats and it's backs against the wall for United.

They're putting pressure on us, breaking up our play, giving us no time on the ball and . . .

. . . Amy starts asking some stupid question.

'Well?' says Amy impatiently.

'Well what?' I ask.

Why can't she just go and watch a video or something?

'When will Mum be home?'

I put my hands over my ears and try to shut her out.

'Oh, I don't know. Soon.'

Mum's still at parents' evening. Dad too. She's summoned him to do his paternal duty. I've been dreading this all week. They'll find out about the booster class . . . and me going down a Maths group . . . and the mock results. In a way I'm kind of hoping they'll have a bit of an argument. At least that way the heat is off me. Oh, what am I saying? That's wrong. Wrong and downright selfish. I want them back together. I want that more than anything. I never thought they'd be apart this long. I mean, Mum and Dad, that's the natural order of things. Like United and Alex Ferguson. But all things pass. Even Fergie. He retires next season. The thought makes me uneasy. It's like the ground is shifting under my feet.

'I don't know why they bother with your parents' evening,' says Amy sulkily. 'They never come home happy.'

'Oh, shut up pipsqueak,' I snap. 'Just because you like school.'

Like it? She *adores* it. Teacher's pet, our Amy. Can I do a job for you, Miss? Can I have some extra homework, Miss? Love you, Miss. Three bags full, Miss.

'*I* get good reports,' says Amy.

Oh, quit it, you little pain. Sheringham's just gone close. We're getting back into the game.

'I get good reports,' I mimic in a nasal, whiny voice.

Amy puts her tongue out and goes back to the living room. At last. United go on the attack again, but the ball runs through to Tommy Sorensen, the Sunderland keeper. I'm just making myself some toast when the front door opens. Mum appears first, followed by Dad. He enters uncertainly, as if he's walking on eggshells. We've got a free kick just outside the area,

30

but I don't get to hear the outcome. Mum stamps over to the radio and turns it off. Dad and I exchange glances. Here it comes.

'I was *so* embarrassed!' she begins.

Sorry.

'Some of your grades have actually gone down. Mr Shooter says you just don't try.'

Sorry.

'You didn't even have the decency to tell me you've been put in a remedial group.'

Sorry, sorry, sorry.

'So what have you got to say for yourself?'

'Sorry.'

And on and on she drones.

'Don't you realise this is GCSE year?'

'Yes I do.'

'Don't you care about your future?'

'Of course I do.'

'Don't you have anything to say?'

'I said I'm sorry.'

'I don't mean you,' says Mum. 'I was talking to your dad.'

And guess what Dad says?

Sorry.

Mum gives an exasperated shriek.

'Can I put the football back on?' I ask.

Mum darts an accusing look at Dad, then throws her arms in the air.

'That's all you two care about,' she says, climbing the stairs to get changed out of her posh, parents' evening clothes, 'eleven men chasing a ball around.'

'Put it on, son,' says Dad. His voice is a strangled whisper.

It's half-time. 0–0. Liverpool are 1–0 up at Man City. Arsenal won last night. If we don't get all three points tonight we'll lose ground in the Championship race.

'Aren't you going to have a go at me, too?' I ask.

'It'd be a bit rich coming from me,' says Dad. 'I didn't do much at school. At least you're good at three subjects.'

'Three?'

'Yes, English, French and IT.'

I never knew I was good at IT.

'So what is it with Maths and Science? Is it because you find the work hard or because you're bored off your box?'

'Both,' I say.

'That's how I was. Don't worry, your mum will calm down.'

'What about you two?' I venture. 'Anything new?'

'No, she still wants the divorce. Looks like it's a done deal.'

'Oh.'

Amy comes in and gives Dad a big hug. He swings her up to the ceiling. She squeals with delight. Life's easy when you're nine.

'I'm going to bed now,' she says. 'Night, Dad.'

'Night, petal.'

She ignores me.

Mum walks back into the kitchen. She's wearing a Bon Bleu jogging suit. I haven't seen her in it for ages. Then I realise why. She stopped wearing it when she developed bumps that shouldn't be there. But the bumps have gone. I've got a new, bumpless Mum.

'You've lost weight,' I gasp.

She forgets she's angry with me long enough to smile.

'Thanks for noticing,' she says.

'I noticed too,' says Dad lamely.

She ignores him completely. Her body language says he's no right to be looking any more.

'I'm making coffee,' says Mum. 'Do you want one, Geoff, or do you have to go?'

The way she says it leaves Dad in no doubt that he ought to go. Immediately.

'No thanks,' he says sadly. 'See you, Sharon. See you, son.'

As Dad closes the front door behind him I realise that this is no temporary separation. It really could be over.

Wednesday 31st January
8.53 p.m.

It's Bobby. He's in his school uniform.

'What are you wearing that for?' I ask, horrified.

'Mum dragged me along to parents' evening,' he says. 'She thought it would look better if I went in uniform. I feel a right prat.'

'You look like one.'

'Thanks for the vote of confidence.'

I'm about to say something else when Paddy Crerand goes ape on the radio commentary.

'1–0 to United. Goal king Cole!'

Andy Cole's put us in the lead.

'Ye-e-e-sssss!'

'And Michael Grey's having a go at the referee. He's off. Michael Grey's been sent off for foul and abusive language.'

'Ye-e-e-sssss!'

United ahead and Sunderland down to ten men. Just what I need after the roasting Mum gave me.

'So how are the Blues doing?' asks Bobby. 'Or shouldn't I ask?'

'You shouldn't ask,' I say sympathetically. 'You're 1–0 down.'

'Liverpool?'

'Were 1–0 up. It's 1–1 now.'

'That's something, I suppose.'

But just as I'm dancing round the room, Andy Cole and Sunderland's Alex Rae square up. It's handbags at forty paces but the ref sends them both off. United down to ten men, Sunderland down to nine. The crowd's going mental. This is crazy.

'Referees,' I say, shaking my head.

'Referees,' says Bobby, rolling his eyes.

He changes the subject.

'Have you spoken to Emma lately?' he asks.

My stomach flips inside out. I know I must have gone red. What's this about?

'We've spoken,' I say guardedly. 'Why?'

'Dunno. Can't quite put my finger on it. She seems a bit lukewarm, that's all. Any idea why?'

How do I answer this? Maybe I should plead the Fifth. In the event I manage a half-decent reply:

'No idea. A slow burn from New Year?'

'Nah. She's forgiven me for that.'

'You sure about that?' I ask.

Bobby squints thoughtfully.

'Has Emma said something?'

'She has mentioned your snog with Pepsey.'

'One slip,' says Bobby indignantly. 'One little mistake. I'd forgive her for one mistake.'

I doubt that, but I don't say so.

He shakes his head.

'Women!' he says.

'Women!' I say, not because I agree with him, but because I want to put him off the scent.

We exchange news.

His love life's gone sour, mine doesn't even exist.

He got a great report, I got . . . a report.

His mum's buying him a new mobile, mine's throwing darts at a picture of me.

'Have you walked under a ladder or something?' he asks.

'Must've,' I say.

'Still, at least United are winning.'

I nod.

Wish I was.

Wednesday 31st January
9.25 p.m.

'Has Bobby gone home?' asks Mum.

'Yes, he cleared off when Middlesborough went 2–1 up.'

'Sorry I lost my temper,' she says. 'I was so disappointed, that's all.'

'You made that pretty clear.'

I'm not in the mood for a heart-to-heart. United and Sunderland are still playing.

'You *will* try though, won't you love?' she asks.

First the roasting, now the guilt trip.

'Yes Mum, I'll try.'

'That's all I want, Terry. Just do your best.'

She's on her way out of the room when I call her back.

'Mum, is it definitely over? You and Dad, I mean?'

There are three minutes left in the match. I want a quick answer.

'It's over,' she says.

'He is sorry,' I say.

'There are some things sorry can't put right.'

I watch her go. United are winning. I'm not. There are four minutes of extra time, four minutes to maintain our lead at the top of the table.

Do it for me, United. My life's going down the tubes, so for God's sake hold on.

Oh no, hand ball on the edge of the area. Barthez saves the free kick. Fifty seconds to go.

Corner to Sunderland. Phillips loops the ball over the bar.

Go on, United. Salvage something out of this mess.

Varga goes for goal for Sunderland. Barthez holds on to the ball. That's it. The full-time whistle goes. Sunderland 0, United 1.

So what if I got a lousy report? So what if Julie's still with Fitz? So what if I'm getting the come-on from my best friend's girl? United are always there like a rock.

Returning the love.

Thursday 1st February
12.45 p.m.

I'm standing outside the canteen holding the umbrella Julie gave me last night. I've been trying to return it all morning. That isn't quite true, I suppose. It's Kelly's umbrella, after all, but I haven't gone near her. No, it's Julie I want to give it to, on condition I catch her on her own. I don't want an audience when I'm making an idiot of myself. All that time I ignored her and now I just want to hear her voice. Bobby comes up with Emma. He sees me holding the umbrella and looks up at the ceiling.

'Where's the leak?'

'What?'

He points to the umbrella.

'It was a joke. At least it was meant to be.'

I just want him to go away, him and Emma. She's putting me in a difficult situation. I haven't forgotten the kiss outside the Sports Hall. My skin burns at the thought of it.

'So when did you start carrying an umbrella?' asks Bobby. 'Not turning into Mary Poppins, are you?'

He puts on a Dick Van Dyke Cockney accent: 'God bless you, Terry Payne.'

For the second time in as many minutes I fail to see the joke.

'It's Kelly's umbrella.'

'So what are *you* doing with it?'

'Julie gave it to me.'

Bobby looks genuinely confused. Emma isn't. She's got the situation sussed straight away. The moment she sees Julie coming down the corridor, she taps Bobby on the arm.

'Let's leave him to it.'

Bobby sees Julie and the penny drops at last.

'I've got the umbrella,' I announce hurriedly as Julie approaches. She's got her long, raven-black hair in a single plait. Her skin appears sun-tanned, but it can't be, not in February. I don't think it's a sunbed tan, either. However she does it, she looks wonderful. All the better for being alone. No Fitz and no Kelly. I hold out the umbrella.

'Thanks.'

She pauses and looks around.

'Was that Bobby and Emma?'

'Yes.'

'So what's going on there?'

'I don't . . .'

I do, but I can't think of a way to explain.

'Bobby and Emma. *You* and Emma. Is this a little love triangle you've got going?'

'There is no *me and Emma*.'

'No? What about outside the Sports Hall? What about New Year?'

'We're friends.'

'Just good friends, eh?'

There's a mischievous twinkle in Julie's eyes.

'I said I'd walk her home from the party. It was a thank-you peck on the cheek.'

I get the feeling that, deep down, she knows that's all there is to it. She's enjoying teasing me.

'And outside the Sports Hall?'

'It was nothing.'

'Does Emma know it's nothing?' says Julie. 'Does *Bobby*?'

I've probably gone bright red by now. If I had a spade I'd dig a hole, jump in and bury myself.

'I told you, there's nothing between me and Emma. Bobby's

my best mate, for goodness' sake! I wouldn't mess with his girl.'

I'm burbling, sinking into a quicksand of embarrassment. And yet Julie's still smiling. Why does she find my discomfort so amusing?

'You're funny,' she says.

'I am?'

I don't feel particularly funny. It's not like I've grown a red nose or a pair of outsize feet.

'It doesn't take much to wind you up, does it?'

'No, clockwork boy, that's me.'

There, done it again, just when I should be explaining what really happened when Fitz broke his ankle, I start telling dumb jokes. Why am I such a wimp?

'Julie . . .'

'Yes?'

'There's something I've got to tell you.'

She smiles broadly. Look at that, I ignore her for a whole month and she still smiles at me. I watch her lips part, and I dissolve inside. Great, my innards are made of Disprol. Any minute, I'll be no more than a fizzy patch on the floor.

'It's about . . .'

Oh no, Kelly's just come out of the canteen with Gary Tudor.

'Go on,' says Julie, obviously intrigued.

And there's Fitz coming the other way with Jamie Sneddon. It's a pincer movement. I look around for an escape route and find it in the shape of the side door that leads outside.

'No,' I say, bolting for freedom. 'It was only that Mum might be looking for a baby-sitter. It doesn't really matter.'

I escape into the frosty air. What do I mean, *doesn't matter*? The most beautiful girl in the world doesn't matter! Of course it matters – more than anything. I didn't want to talk to her about baby-sitting. If only she knew what really happened between me and Fitz. I didn't set out to hurt him. He was going to get me. I haven't got an aggressive bone in my body. Well, except for this sudden desire to beat Fitz's brains out with Kelly's umbrella!

Thursday 1st February
8.00 p.m.

'Terry!'

I hear Mum calling me, but I don't really register. Her voice comes through a dream haze. I've been thinking about Julie. I see her the way I saw her the first time, in the gym, in that royal blue leotard . . . running. Boy, was she running! It was rhythmic, mesmerising, soft-focus running. I'm supposed to be doing my homework, but I'm seeing that back tuck of hers in glorious slow motion, and I'm doodling her name over and over again on my jotter. Julie, Julie, Julie.

'Terry!'

Mum's still not punching through the dream haze. Blue leotards take precedence over harrassed mums any day of the week.

'Terry!'

I look up. Mum and Amy and her best mate Katie are standing next to me.

'What?'

'I've been shouting for you for half an hour.'

I frown. She's got to be exaggerrating.

'OK, about a minute, but why don't you answer?'

'That's why,' says Amy, snatching the jotter off me. 'Terry's in lurrvve.'

'Give that back!'

Amy skips out of reach.

'Mum, tell her to give it back.'

A torrent of emotions rages through me: embarrassment, anger, humiliation.

'What's it say?' asks Katie. Her eyes widen. 'Julie Carter! She's my baby-sitter.'

More emotions: interest, passion, panic.

What if Katie rats on me? I'd never be able to look Julie in the face again.

'Yours!'

'Yes, she's been doing it for ages, since before Christmas.'

I remember that Katie lives in Huyton, near the Bluebell. Not ten minutes from Julie's house. It could be true.

'Wait till I tell her.'

I make a grab for my jotter. I snatch it back at the second time of asking.

'Don't!'

'Oh Katie, you've got to,' chuckles Amy.

I fix Katie with pleading eyes.

'Please.'

I feel like the wuss of the century. I'm pleading with a nine-year-old. How sad is that? It comes out *Purr-leese*.

'What's it worth?' asks Amy.

Mum laughs.

'Mum,' I groan. 'Tell her.'

Mum smiles.

'Don't get so uptight. Nobody's going to rumble you, Terry. Amy and Katie are just winding you up.'

'You won't tell, will you?' I say, the slightest hint of a shake in my voice.

Katie pulls a face, as if weighing up her options.

'Your secret's safe with us,' smirks Amy in that flesh-creepingly superior way of hers.

'If you girls have stopped teasing Terry,' Mum says, 'I'd like you to get in the car.'

She squeezes my shoulder. 'That's what I was trying to tell you. We'll be about half an hour.'

'OK,' I croak, dying inside.

I hear the door go. I stare at the doodles on my jotter. How could I be so stupid? My fate is in the hands of a nine-year-old. Could I be more vulnerable?

4

This morning's *Daily Mirror* got me thinking. If United can team up with the New York Yankees, maybe that's what I need; a collaboration. I can just see it: Terry Payne meets Romeo, Ginger Nut links up with Casanova, Mad Manc joins forces with David Beckham. Let's face it, it's the only way I'm going to get anywhere with Julie, especially if Katie drops her bombshell. It doesn't seem to matter what I do, the result's the same every rotten time, the mathematics of misery.

Terry Payne minus Julie Carter equals heartache.

Julie Carter plus John Fitzpatrick equals jealousy.

As for Terry Payne plus Julie Carter, that would quite simply add up to heaven on earth. It would also be a miracle.

'What are you grinning at?' asks Amy, noticing the Julie-induced smile.

She always moans on footy practice night. I can't blame her.

Ever since Mum started working late, I've had to pick Amy up from her school and drag her down to Knowsley Manor.

She has to shiver her socks off for an hour while I train. Next week's an away fixture and Mum has actually been wondering whether Amy can go on the bus with the team! I told her it was a non-starter. Six Guns – Mr Shooter – would go ballistic at the thought of it. He isn't exactly crazy about me having to drag her along to practice every week.

'Can't condemn a man for smiling,' I say.

'But what are you smiling *about*?' asks Amy.

'Wouldn't you like to know?'

I can't resist teasing her.

'You're stupid!' she says. 'I'm going to tell Mum on you.'

40

'So,' I say, ignoring my own advice, 'tell her.'

Now wasn't that mature! Amy pouts.

'If I say you've been horrible to me, she'll stop you going to football. You'll just have to take me home instead. Or . . .'

She gives her superior smirk.

'I'll get Katie to tell Julie about you.'

Damn! I forgot Amy had the whip hand. One word from her and I'm dead. Another victory for Fitz. There's only one way to sort this. Bribery.

'OK, what do you want?'

Amy scratches her chin theatrically. She wants to keep me hanging on.

'Dunno. You'll have to make it worth my while.'

'Come on, I know you've got something in mind.'

'Well, there is this art magazine. I saw it on telly. It shows you how to shade fruit.'

'Go on, how much?'

'Three pounds.'

'Three quid!'

I could shade gold bullion for that!

'So should I have a word with Katie?'

'Don't you dare!'

But Amy knows when she's on to a winner. No amount of shouting is going to put her off. She cuts me short with a cheeky: 'Bribe please.'

We nip into the newsagents by the school gates. When we come out Amy is one art magazine richer, I'm three pounds poorer. That leaves me with one pound fifty to last till Friday. It isn't a complete disaster though.

The two-minute delay buying Amy's stupid magazine means we walk in on a full-blown row between Julie and Fitz. What's three pounds compared to the promise of heaven? We're too far away to catch the drift, but it's obvious that not everything's hunky-dory in paradise. After a couple of minutes Julie throws her hands up and storms off. I watch the long legs, the black, swinging ponytail. If only . . . if only . . .

'Quick,' I hiss, shoving Amy round the corner of the Sports Hall, 'she's coming this way.'

'Hey, stop pushing!'

'Amy, please,' I beg, 'pipe down.'

Julie breaks into a run. Her hair whips up off her shoulders like the tail of a black panther. I watch, enthralled. I've been crazy about her for months and still the thrill of seeing her hasn't faded a bit. She's half the reason I get out of bed in the morning. Man U's the other half.

'Run Julie run,' I murmur.

Amy gives me a funny look. Brain to mouth: turn down the volume.

'Julie,' Fitz calls after her. 'Don't go. I didn't mean it.'

He's about to say something else when he notices me and Amy watching him. He goes bright red.

'What's the matter with you, MnM?' he snarls.

I've rarely seen him looking so uncomfortable. I wish this moment could last for ever.

'Nothing,' I say, revelling in the reversal of fortunes. 'Nothing at all.'

Wednesday 7th February
8.00 p.m.

I'm sitting on a wall with Bobby.

'What's the matter with you?' he asks. 'I thought you'd be over the moon. Julie and Frisky Fitzy at each other's throats, what more could you want?'

'Nothing.'

'So why the long face?'

'I think I'll have to miss the next match.'

Mum's just broken the news.

'Why?'

I bury my chin deep in my jacket.

'It's away. I've got to look after our Amy. It's OK taking her along to Knowsley Manor but she can't come on the minibus to an away match. Six Guns won't stand for it.'

'What about your mum and dad?'

'Both working late.'

'There's got to be somebody.'

There is. Julie. But I couldn't ask her. I wouldn't dare.

'Grandparents?' says Bobby.

I shake my head.

'No go. I'm snookered. Just when I'd got Fitz's place in the side.'

'I could baby-sit.'

'You!'

'I'm not in the team any more, and my band's broken up.'

His band was called *The Sons of Mo Szyslak*. There are two theories about why they broke up. One is musical differences, the other is Bobby lusting after the drummer's girlfriend.

'Why shouldn't I baby-sit?'

Because it would be like putting an arsonist in charge of a firework factory, that's why!

'I don't think Mum would fancy you doing it. She hasn't forgiven you for the time she caught you smoking in our bathroom.'

'It was only the once. I don't do it any more.'

'It was once too often.'

Bobby ponders for a moment or two.

'Got it,' he says.

His face lights up. It's an Archimedes and bathwater moment.

'Emma! She'll do it.'

I remember Emma nudging along the bench, pressing close to me, the smell of her hair, her perfume, the touch of her lips. All that stuff about going out with the wrong mate. No, that really would be asking for trouble.

'No,' I say, rather too hastily, 'not Emma.'

Bobby's face clouds over.

'Why not?'

Yes, why not? Think, Terry lad, think. An excuse, I need an excuse. But what?

'She's your girlfriend.'

'Meaning?'

Yes, what do I mean? Trust me to blurt that out. I've given the game away this time. Come on, there's got to be something I can say. Not just anything, either. It's got to be watertight. No sieve-style explanations.

Got it!

'I don't want you inviting yourself round. I can just imagine it. There's you and Emma snogging in the living room and our Amy walks in. Mum would hit the roof.'

It works. If there's one thing that's guaranteed to work on Bobby, it's flattery. He likes nothing better than being portrayed as some sort of love god.

'Aw, you've got me sussed. Anyway, there must be other baby-sitters.'

'There is one,' I say doubtfully.

'Who?'

'Julie.'

'*The* Julie? She baby-sits?'

I nod.

'This is destiny,' Bobby gasps. 'It's got to be.'

'No,' I say. 'It's stupid.'

Bobby shakes his head.

'Why is it? Stop being such a wuss. Just ask her.'

I look at him, allowing hope to flare.

'I could, couldn't I?'

Friday 9th February
7.00 p.m.

Masterplan about to be put into practice. I'm standing in the kitchen trying to look cool. This is good, I'm leaning against the fridge, swigging from a can of Red Bull and flicking through a GCSE Study Guide. It's just the right balance to strike. Nonchalant *and* studious. But will Mum buy it? Oh, hurry up. Phone Julie. She's had the number since yesterday when I handed it to her. I didn't ask Julie, of course, I couldn't pluck up the courage. I'm hoping Mum will do the job for me. She's phoned Katie's mum. I think she got a good reference. I'm determined not to remind her about it. I don't want to sound too keen. Not good for the image. Besides, she'll smell a rat and get another baby-sitter instead, somebody with braces and a wooden leg.

This weird little alien voice fills my head:

'E.T. Phone Julie.'

Then it goes frantic.

'E.T. Phone Julie, phone Julie, phone Ju-leeee!'

'Do you remember where I put that phone number?' Mum asks.

This is it. Sound unconcerned.

44

'What number's that?'

'You know which number. Julie the baby-sitter, the one you've got a crush on.'

Ouch. I've been rumbled.

'It's by the phone.'

'You sure?'

I should be, I put it there.

Mum goes into the hall.

'Here it is. It fell behind the phone table.'

I make a mental note. Next time Blutak it to the stupid table. Nail it down if you have to.

I hold my breath as Mum punches the number.

'Oh, hello. Is Julie there?'

Please be in, please be in, please be in.

'Julie? Hi, this is Mrs Payne.'

She's in! I punch the air. Yiss!

'That's right, Terry's mum.'

There's a pause, while Julie asks a question. That's right, be suspicious!

'That's right,' says Mum. 'Terry suggested you.'

I find myself edging towards the kitchen door. Say you'll do it, Julie, *please* say you will.

'You can. Oh, that's such a relief. Boys and their football.'

Mum laughs at something Julie's said. Oh no, don't say they're laughing at me!

'That's arranged then. Our Terry will take you to the school to pick up Amy, you know, introduce the pair of you . . . Oh, you have. Well it won't hurt for you both to meet her the first time. Then he'll go off to his football and you'll bring Amy home.'

It's a ten or fifteen minute walk from my school to Amy's. That means Julie and me together all that time. There's a lump in my throat the size of a duck's egg. Masterplan complete.

When Mum hangs up I fly back to my station and continue flicking through the Study Guide. OK, so she knows Julie the baby-sitter and Julie the crush are one and the same, but at least I can try to look cool.

'It's all fixed up,' says Mum. 'Oh, and by the way, your book's upside down!'

45

There's Julie. She's just ahead of me, making her way through the crowd of kids at the school gates.

'Are you still on for tomorrow night?' I ask, catching her up.

It's a miracle. She's on her own. No Kelly and no Fitz either. Both her minders have gone AWOL. Come to think of it, I haven't seen her with Fitz for days. Mentally, I cross my fingers.

'Yes,' says Julie with a smile.

She gives a low, throaty chuckle.

'Just like I was still on yesterday and the day before.'

You idiot, Terry, I tell myself. You're coming across all desperate again.

'I was just checking,' I say, trying to recover. 'I don't want anything going wrong, you know, with Amy.'

'I know exactly what you mean,' says Julie, emphasising the *exactly*.

She looks right at me, through me, and I dissolve in her lush, brown eyes.

'Sorry,' I say.

'What are you saying sorry for?' she asks.

Anything you want.

Sorry for being a pest.

Sorry for having ginger hair.

Sorry for being thick.

Sorry for being a Mad Manc.

Sorry for not being good enough for you.

But I'm not sorry for loving you.

'Dunno,' I say with a nervous giggle. 'Sorry.'

She laughs too. It's a lovely sound. There is nothing cruel or malicious about her. She can tease me without humiliating me. I can't believe how strongly I feel about this girl.

'So I'll see you at home-time tomorrow,' she says. 'And we'll pick Amy up together.'

There's a hidden goodbye in there somewhere. Then I see the reason why. Kelly is jogging towards us, so much like Sabrina, the Teenage Witch, I can almost feel myself turning into a frog. I watch them walking away together. Kelly turns to Julie as if to say: I don't know why you give him the time of day.

Neither do I.

But I'm glad she does.

Tuesday 13th February
8.30 p.m.

'Stupid men!' says Mum as she walks through the front door.

She's been to the supermarket with Amy. As they start to pack the shopping away, I venture a cautious:

'Why are men stupid?'

I figure I might learn something about the female mind. I'm not too good on all that Venus and Mars stuff. I'm astronomically challenged.

'You should have seen them,' says Mum. 'Queuing up with their Valentine's Day love baskets. All with the same, pathetic, embarrassed look on their faces.'

Valentine's Day! Of course, tomorrow's Valentine's Day.

'And not one of them means it. They only do it to stay out of the dog-house.'

'How do you know they don't mean it?' I ask.

I'm not defending the male species, just this particular member of it.

'Your dad didn't mean it, did he? Bought me flowers every Valentine's Day for seventeen years, then he just walked out on a whim. So much for romance.'

She finishes putting the shopping away. Pasta, vegetables, low-fat this and hi-fibre that, but not a Hobnob or a Crunchie in sight. The diet continues. I look at her. She's definitely losing weight.

'You're getting thin,' I say.

I'm not sure I like it. Mum's always been cuddly, lived in. Now that the fat's moved out, she looks different, and I don't just mean thinner.

'Good,' she says, 'and I'm going to get even thinner, with your help.'

'My help?'

'That's right. I've joined a running club. Monday and Friday evenings, seven till nine. You're baby-sitting. Don't worry, I'll pay you.'

'What if I want to go out?' I ask.

'Simple,' says Mum with a twinkle in her eye. 'I can always phone Julie.'

Mum thin, Mum running, Julie in my house. It's a brave new world and I'm not sure I can cope with it. I'm on my way upstairs when my mobile goes.

'Oh, hi Dad.'

'I rang you on your mobile so your mum didn't hear. Are we safe to talk?'

I carry on into my room. Privacy among the litter.

'Yes, fire away. Is it about tomorrow night?'

I mean the match. Champions' League. United v. Valencia in Spain.

'Yes.'

Only Dad isn't talking about football, as I discover from his next sentence.

'I got your mum a Valentine's Day present.'

'You're joking!'

'Why?'

'Because she doesn't want to know. You'll only make things worse.'

'She always liked a bit of romance.'

Dad, I think, groaning inwardly, don't do this to yourself.

'What have you got her?'

It can't be what I'm thinking.

'I picked it up at the supermarket.'

Dad, you dufus.

'It's called a love basket.'

Basket-case is more like it.

'Do you think it's worth a try?' he asks.

'Sure,' I say, 'If you fancy open-heart surgery without anaesthetic.'

'That bad, huh?'

'Dad, you don't know the half of it.'

There's a long silence at the other end.

'Are you coming over to watch the match?' he asks plaintively.

I don't really want to commit myself. What if Julie's in no hurry to go after baby-sitting?

'Terry?'

I'd be a mug to go to Dad's.

'I'll be there,' I tell him.

I know, I'm a mug. But at least I'm a loyal mug, a mug who can look himself in the mirror in the morning.

Wednesday 14th February
12.20 p.m.

'Have you got Emma anything?' I ask Bobby as we walk past the shops.

He grins.

'A big, sloppy kiss.'

'Anything else?'

'Yes, I got her a card. A rude one.'

'How rude?'

'Oh, a real cheek-slapper.'

'What did she think of it?'

'Dunno. I haven't given it to her yet.'

He fishes it out of his blazer pocket and hands it to me. I read it.

'You can't give her that!'

'Why not?'

'She's a nice girl.'

I remember the way she snuggled up close. Are nice girls supposed to do *that* to their boyfriend's best mate?

'Why do you ask?'

I take a deep breath. Here goes nothing.

'I was thinking of buying Julie something.'

'Is this why you dragged me out of school for dinner?' asks Bobby.

I give an embarrassed nod.

'What were you thinking of getting her?'

'That's just it, I haven't got a clue. I thought you might have some suggestions.'

I give him his card back. Those sort of suggestions I don't need. We find ourselves outside a florist's. It's heaving with bouquets and balloons, hearts and teddy bears. I look at some of the price tags. My heart sinks.

'Dear, aren't they?' says Bobby.

I nod miserably. I couldn't afford a ventricle, never mind a whole heart.

'Come on, let's get back.'

We're turning to go when Fitz makes an unwelcome appearance.

'What's this, MnM, buying something for your Valentine?'

Gary's with him. He chips in with his two-pennyworth:

'Bobby, you're a lucky guy.'

'A match made in heaven,' says Fitz.

Before we can stop him, he's pinched both our cheeks.

'You young lovebirds!'

Then he's gone.

'If Julie's ditched him,' Bobby says, rubbing his cheek, 'he's taking it well.'

There are a few rose petals on the pavement. I watch them blow away, just like my dreams.

Wednesday 14th February
3.15 p.m.

'OK,' says Julie, appearing out of a scrum of kids, 'I'm all yours.'

My heart lurches. If only that were true. I notice Kelly glaring at me. What's the matter, somebody step on your wand?

'See you later, Julie,' she says.

We turn right. She turns left. She must hate leaving Julie with me. The Scouse princess and the Mad Manc.

'How's your gymnastics going?' I ask.

'Great. We've started training three times a week.'

'Three!'

'Yes, Tuesdays, Thursdays and Saturdays.'

'It must take dedication.'

'I suppose it does,' says Julie. 'I'm used to it now. It's just like doing homework.'

I grimace.

'I wouldn't really know about that.'

'You're not keen on school, are you?'

I shake my head.

'So what are you doing next year?'

'I'm going to college,' I answer. 'Can't wait to get away from this place.'

I wince. That came out wrong. There's at least one person I don't want to get away from.

'What about you?' I ask.

'I'm going into sixth form,' she says, 'so long as I get the grades.'

'You'll get the grades,' I say. 'You're dead clever.'

She laughs, completely unaffected.

'Thanks.'

I'm dying to ask her, what about Fitz? I do it in my usual roundabout way.

'Had any Valentines?'

'A few.'

A **few**! So I'm not Fitz's only rival . . .

'You?'

How do I answer this?

'Oh, you know, one or two.'

'Is that one or two?' she asks, smiling.

'None,' I mumble.

I'm not sure honesty is the best policy.

'Aw, poor Terry.'

Funnily enough, she sounds like she means it. We've almost reached Amy's school. The time has flashed by in an instant. I had so much to say, too. But it will have to remain unsaid.

'There's your Amy now,' says Julie.

I nod.

'See you then.'

I don't move.

'Haven't you got to get back?'

I just stare dumbly.

'The match.'

I look at my watch. I've got to be on the bus in ten minutes.

'I'll see you later,' I say, turning to go. 'See you, Amy.'

By the time they answer, I'm running back towards Knowsley Manor.

51

Wednesday 14th February
6.20 p.m.

As I turn into our street, my heart is pounding. I've run all the way from school, a mixture of elation, hope and excitement. The elation was provided by a 3–0 win. I made one and scored one. Julie's providing the rest. When I get to the door I fumble for my keys and drop them on the pavement. By the time I've retrieved them, somebody has opened the front door.

Let it be Julie.

It isn't.

'Oh, it's you.'

'Who did you expect?' asks Amy. 'Oh, I get it. You thought Julie would still be here.'

'You mean she's gone?'

'Half an hour ago, when Mum came in.'

I follow Amy inside and throw my bag on the floor.

'Temper, temper,' says Amy.

By way of reply, I scowl.

'That you, Terry?' asks Mum.

'No, the Amazing Spiderman.'

'Well,' Mum quips in return, 'spin your web into the kitchen. Something came in the post.'

'For me?'

'Yes Terry, for you.'

'What is it?'

'How should I know? Do you think I steam your letters open?'

The moment I walk into the kitchen, my heart does a somersault. It's a card. In a red envelope.

A Valentine's Day card.

I open it and read:

'To a nice guy. Lots of love.'

I try to remember what Julie's writing looks like, but I don't remember ever seeing it. I scrutinise the message for hidden meanings.

A nice guy . . .

. . . lots of . . .

. . . love!

Lots of, not just bits of.

Let it be from her. *Please* let it be from her.

Wednesday 14th February
7.20 p.m.

Though it has been frosty all day, I walk to Dad's flat embalmed in a warm glow.

I see the message on the card. Lots of love!

'You look pleased with yourself,' Dad says when he answers the door.

'I got a Valentine,' I explain. 'From *her*.'

'Oh, this Julie you've been telling me about.'

'I think it's from her.'

It's got to be. Who else would send me one?

'At least one of us has had a Valentine,' says Dad glumly.

I spot the love basket sitting on the coffee table. The rose petals are already withering, and the little teddy bear looks like he's seen better days.

'You didn't send it then?'

Dad shakes his head.

'No. You were right. Sharon would only have lost her temper. There's no point making things even worse. I'd better face it, this divorce is a done deal. I'll be a free man any day now.'

He smiles unconvincingly, then admits:

'Can't say I'm looking forward to it much.'

I imagine him fishing in the Meals for One cabinet at the supermarket. For the want of anything better to say I tell him:

'Mum's taking up jogging.'

Dad does a double-take.

'Is this the same Sharon Payne we're talking about?'

'I'm not making it up. Every Monday and Friday. She's lost loads of weight with the diet. Once she starts running there'll be nothing left.'

Dad stands with his mouth open, like a codfish in slow motion. It's really starting to sink in now. He's beginning to understand just what he's thrown away.

'Have you got the right channel on?' I ask.

'Yes. It'll be starting any minute.'

We settle in front of the TV just in time to hear the strains of

53

the Champions' League anthem. I listen while Des Lynam sets the scene. Mestalla stadium . . . bucketing down all day . . . water lying on the pitch.

Then the size of the task before United: Valencia have the best defensive record in the competition; they are unbeaten at home by foreign opposition since 1992; United have never beaten a Spanish side on their own soil. We're playing last year's runners-up on their own turf. It isn't going to be easy.

'Don't worry,' says Dad, sensing my anxiety. 'We took four points off them last year.'

Weird how, when it really matters, all we can talk about is football. That laminated leather ball must have been designed to fill the hole where men's feelings ought to go. The match gets off to a cracking start. Both sides are going for it. After five minutes Giggsy nutmegs a defender and finds Cole in the box. After ten Valencia put the ball in the net, but it is ruled offside. Twenty minutes in, Beckham almost gets on the end of a Giggs cross.

'Giggsy's got the beating of Angloma,' says Dad.

But on the half-hour it's Valencia who are turning the screw. During a period of relentless pressure Wes Brown denies Mendietta. Two minutes later Scholes comes close with a great half-volley. Two heavyweights are throwing bombs at each other, but at half-time it's still 0–0.

'Let's just take a look at those terrific wins for Leeds and Arsenal last night,' says Des Lynam.

'Let's get a snack,' says Dad, rocketing out of his chair like it's an ejector seat.

No self-respecting Red is going to sit around and watch the opposition do well. It's only fun watching Liverpool, Leeds or Arsenal when they lose.

'Are you wishing you could turn back the clock?' I ask. 'Over Mum I mean?'

'I never think of anything else,' says Dad. 'I can't live down my mistake. It's with me every minute of every day.'

'So why did you walk out in the first place?'

'You really want to know?'

'Yes.'

'What set me off was this lad at work. He got divorced and met a girl ten years younger. I envied him. I mean, it was all routine with your mum. I only started to realise that I needed our routine when I moved out.'

Dad shakes his head.

'I'm one brain-dead plank.'

So who's arguing?

By the time we return to the living room it's the new Budweiser advert.

In unison we chorus: 'Wassup!' then laugh, like it's original.

'Want to put a bet on the score?' asks Dad.

'No.'

It would be tempting fate.

'Here's my prediction, for what it's worth,' says Dad. '1–0 to United.'

But with half an hour to go it is Aimar and Mendietta for Valencia who are starting to boss the game. It's a Thrilla at the Mestalla, a game of slick, one-touch passing with half-chances by the bucketful. But at the full-time whistle there is still no score.

'A draw will suit United,' says Dad. 'One more win and we're through to the quarter-finals.'

'That'll do me,' I say, with more than a hint of satisfaction in my voice.

'So this Julie, are you really serious about her?' asks Dad.

'I'd like to be. I don't know how she feels though.'

'Well, don't just stand there wishing,' says Dad. 'Decide what you want and go for it.'

I give a half-smile.

'Yes, I know it's a bit rich coming from me, but it's good advice all the same.'

I walk to the door.

'Think about it, Terry,' says Dad.

I already have. I'm going to phone Julie on the way home.

Wednesday 14th February
9.45 p.m.

I try her mobile. It's switched off. Great. Now I've got to ring her at home. I daren't postpone this. I'll never pluck up the courage again. I listen to the ringing tone. Getting Julie is a six to one shot. Any of them could pick up. Her mum, her dad, one of her three brothers: Gerard, Josh or John-Joe. If I get Julie it's got to be a sign; destiny.

I listen to it ring.

Let it be her, please let it be her.

Somebody picks up and speaks.

It **is** her. Oh my God, what do I do now? What on earth do I say? Why didn't I plan this better?

'Hello?'

Tell her you love her, you wimp.

'Hello?'

Say it. *Say something.*

'Is that you, Fitz?'

What do I say?

My mind races through the possibilities:

I love you? Too dramatic.

I care? Too needy.

Do you want to go out with me? Too ordinary.

I'm trying to come up with more permutations when Julie loses patience. She hangs up. I stand at the top of our street, beating my head with the mobile.

One of the neighbours is out walking his dog. He gives me ever such a funny look. The dog's suspicious too.

I'm about to go through the front door when I notice I've got a text message. The words make a chill run down my spine:

Did U like my card? Emma.

Emma!

Emma sent me the Valentine!

I stare at the mobile in disbelief. I've just come within a hair's breadth of making a complete idiot of myself.

5

'You mean you hung up without saying *anything*!'

I've just told Bobby about the abortive phone call to Julie. I keep quiet about Emma's text message and the Valentine, of course.

'You've got to get in there, Terry lad, before somebody beats you to it.'

'You've lost me.'

'Do you walk about in a daze or something? It's the talk of Year 11. Julie's finally done it, she's given Fitz the heave-ho.'

I always thought that, when their break-up finally happened, it would be a real big deal. There would be advance warning, then a huge, theatrical bust-up followed by an extensive post-mortem. We're talking sirens and lights, crashing waves, thunderbolts and lightning. In the event, the Fitz and Julie roadshow just got shunted quietly into the sidings.

'Are you sure about this?' I ask.

My voice has gone all quavery.

'Sure I'm sure.'

'Then how do you explain that?'

Fitz's posse has just come round the corner. There's Gary Tudor, Kelly Magee, Paul Scully, Pepsey Cooper, Jamie Sneddon and . . . Julie.

'I said her and Fitz had stopped going out. I didn't say they were mortal enemies.'

This I find hard to take. I've heard about people staying friends when they break up. I didn't think it actually happened. It's certainly not like that with Mum and Dad. Amy and I feel like we're tip-toeing round emotional razor wire.

As the group walk past I catch Julie's eye. I give a half-smile. It sets Fitz off.

'What are you grinning at, MnM?' he snaps, eyes bulging with anger.

I take his over-the-top reaction as proof of Bobby's news.

'See.'

I watch them as they head for double Maths. Julie glances over her shoulder at me.

'What more do you want?' asks Bobby. 'See the way she looked at you? Fitz is history. Go for it.'

Thursday 15th February
12.50 p.m.

I eat my dinner with Bobby and Emma.

'I don't know why it's such a big deal,' says Emma. 'Julie's dumped Fitz. So what?'

'What Emma says seems to make sense,' says Bobby. 'After all, people make love one hundred and twenty million times around the world every day.'

I meet Emma's look and feel distinctly uncomfortable. No way are we going to make it one hundred and twenty million and one!

'But,' says Bobby, oblivious of the exchange of glances, 'there's nothing ordinary about a man in love.'

Oh God Bobby, pass the sick bag.

'Terry's been carrying a major torch for Julie for months. It's a big deal to him.'

'I can't see why,' says Emma, a bit too huffily for my liking. 'She's not so wonderful. Her bum's too big.'

Mee-ow!

'Just drop it, will you?' I say.

Actually, I think Julie's got the world's number one bum. The bum to die for.

'Happy to,' says Bobby. 'By the way, I didn't tell you my news, did I?'

'What news is this?'

'Slughead's proposed to Mum.'

I picture Bobby's Mum's boyfriend. Big guy. Cocker spaniel.

'When?'

'Valentine's Day. They went out for a curry and he poppadomed the question.'

I pass over the stupid pun.

'So how do you feel?'

'How do you think I feel?' says Bobby. 'Gutted. The guy's a complete moron. And he's got sweaty feet. His socks stink the house out. Plus he's a Liverpool fan.'

It's something Bobby and I have in common, our hatred of all things Liverpool, him from an Everton perspective, me from a Man U one.

'What difference does that make?' asks Emma.

'All the difference,' says Bobby. 'And his dog hates me. It puked in my bed.'

I try not to dwell on images of a vomiting spaniel.

'So when's the wedding?' I ask, also trying not to make eye contact with Emma.

'Next month, I think. Registry office do. But he's moving into our house permanently this week.'

Bobby glances at his watch.

'Anyway, I've got to go. I've got IT.'

Emma and I have Maths. Booster Maths.

'See you later.'

'Poor Bobby,' I say.

'Poor Bobby nothing,' says Emma. 'Slughead . . . I mean, Phil, he's OK.'

'And the cocker spaniel?'

'Poor little thing. She had an upset stomach. Lady wouldn't puke in Bobby's bed on purpose.'

We're wittering on aimlessly like this when Julie and Kelly walk by. Julie gives Emma a sideways glance and carries on out of the canteen. I get a sinking feeling.

'I just know she thinks there's something going on between us,' I say.

'Maybe we should really give her something to think about,' says Emma, putting her hand on mine.

I snatch my hand away as if she's just touched me with a cattle prod.

'Emma!'

She smiles mischievously.

'Time for Maths,' she says. 'Coming?'

I follow reluctantly. Like a man on his way to the electric chair.

Thursday 15th February
1.45 p.m.

I'm on my way to Electronic Products when I bump into Julie. From somewhere I get a sudden attack of boldness.

'Is it true about you and Fitz?' I ask.

This simple sentence is the culmination of hours of agonising: ask her, don't ask her, ask her, don't ask her . . . In the event, I can't believe I've actually asked her.

'Yes, it's true. Why?'

Did she have to ask me that?

'No reason. Just being nosy, that's all.'

No! That isn't all. Tell her, you dope. Say how you feel.

'I never thought you were right for each other.'

'No?' says Julie.

'No.'

I thank my lucky stars she didn't go all sarcastic, you know, ask me when I became a Relate counsellor. But the monosyllabic question has thrown me. Now what? I stand, shifting my feet. In the end, I come up with this:

'There's nothing between me and Emma, you know.'

'Did I say there was?' asks Julie.

'No, but . . .'

Maybe I'm protesting too much. Why did I have to say that anyway? There can only be one reason for telling her that. So why not go the whole hog? I can almost hear Bobby's voice: ask her out, for crying out loud! But before I can open my mouth, Julie says something that completely disarms me.

'I should never have gone out with Fitz. Don't get me wrong, he's a great guy . . .'

I bite my bottom lip. This, I don't want to hear. He's not a great guy. If the world had an armpit, its name would be Fitz.

'But I knew weeks ago it wasn't working.'

This, I do want to hear.

'I think I'm going to take my time before I jump into another relationship.'

No, you were doing so well. Don't spoil it.

'Anyway, I've got to get to my next class.'

And, with a turn and a whiff of perfume and a flick of the ponytail she's gone. She doesn't need another relationship! Have I been reading the signs all wrong? Doesn't she like me *at all*?

I stand in the corridor for a long time.

A *very* long time.

Thursday 15th February
11.30 p.m.

I'm in bed, but I can't sleep.

I've made up my mind. Tomorrow I do it. It's the last day before half-term so I've got to do it, or else lose a whole week of my life.

Tomorrow I ask Julie out.

Friday 16th February
11.30 p.m.

In bed again, still unable to sleep.

I messed up. I saw Julie three times but I didn't once ask her out.

I hate me.

6

Monday 19th February
11 a.m.

I've just crawled out of bed. The house is empty. Mum took
Amy round to Katie's on her way to work. The sneakiest nine-
year-old blackmailer in Prescot is spending the day there. On
her way out Mum shouted something about me not sleeping
the day away. I was going to get up about ten, but as soon as I
heard that I stayed between the sheets an extra hour, just to
spite her.

Stupid Mum.

Stupid half-term.

Most of all, stupid ME.

Six months I've spent kicking myself for not asking Julie out.
Now I'm repeating the same pathetic mistake all over again.
Maybe I should ask somebody else to kick me. It might make
more of an impression.

'Pillock!' I say loudly.

I pass the hall mirror.

'Pillock!' I say again, this time with feeling.

I'm also a hungry pillock, so I get myself a bowl of Shreddies.
I notice an official-looking letter on the kitchen table. I run my
eyes over it. It's Mum and Dad's divorce. It's through. The end
of an era. Or is it the end of an error? I'm licking the sweet
gunge from the bottom of the bowl, consoling myself with
sugar, when the doorbell rings.

It's Bobby.

'Emma's two-timing me,' he announces, walking right past
me.

'Morning Bobby,' I say, by way of reminding him about his
manners, and also to give myself time to think.

'Did you hear what I just said?' he demands irritably. 'Emma's seeing someone else.'

I feel like I've gone all red and blotchy. After all, it's me she's seeing, or would be if I'd agree to see her back. This is crazy, week after week I've been doing the decent thing and it looks like I'm still going to get slaughtered.

'How do you know?' I ask nervously.

And *how much* do you know?

Bobby takes a quick swig from the can of Coke he's taken from the fridge, and answers.

'Caitlin told me.'

Caitlin is Bobby's ex. She dumped him when she found out about his other girlfriend, Rosie. Well, you would, wouldn't you?

'Caitlin did!'

'Yes, she couldn't wait to spill the beans. It's the first time she's spoken to me since the split, and didn't she come over all smug and superior! You know what she said: *What goes around, comes around.*'

'Meaning?'

'Meaning I'm getting a dose of my own medicine. And I damned well deserve it.'

I feel like carnivorous worms are eating me alive, from the inside.

'Did she say who it was?'

He takes another swig of Coke. The tension kicks in. I lean forward, dreading what he'll say next.

'No.'

Phew. Relief sweeps through me like Olbas Oil through a blocked nose.

'But,' says Bobby, and it sounds like a big but, 'Caitlin says mine wasn't the only Valentine Emma sent. She's sweet on somebody.'

I see something new in Bobby. He's always been one of these *All's fair in love and war* types. He has never really cared how things were going in a relationship. He could always find somebody else. This time he's angry. No, not angry. *Incandescent.* I'm wondering how to point out that he has cheated on three girls this year, including Emma, when he says:

'I know what you're thinking. I did the dirty on Emma,

snogging Pepsey like that, so what have I got to whinge about?'

Couldn't have put it better myself. Bobby looks at me, misery written in his eyes. How can I tell him the truth? It would be like kicking a puppy.

'Well, you're right. I've been a pig. But when I nearly lost Emma at New Year I started to realise how much she means to me.'

I don't believe it. Bobby's sounding just like Dad!

'Whoever it is,' he says. 'I'll kill him.'

Some week this is turning out to be. Mum and Dad have just got divorced, Liverpool and Arsenal both won, I've failed dismally to make any progress with Julie, and now my best mate is on the trail of the object of Emma's desire – me!

'Are you sure you're not getting this way out of proportion?' I ask. 'I mean, what's a Valentine? People send them for a laugh.'

'Well, this is no joke,' says Bobby, agony twisting through his voice. 'I'm going to find out who's messing about with my girl, and when I do . . .'

He doesn't finish the sentence. Instead, he crushes his Coke can.

'He'll wish he'd never been born.'

I close my eyes for a moment. Don't worry Bobby, he already does!

Tuesday 20th February
11.45 a.m.

We're at the Blue Planet Aquarium. As a concession for half-term, Mum and Dad have each booked a day off work. Today is Dad's day. He told me and Amy we could both bring a friend. Amy asked Katie. I made an excuse about Bobby. I'm kind of avoiding him at the moment. The thought of him finding out exactly who Emma has the hots for has me squirming in my socks.

'So what's Bobby doing again?' asks Dad as we watch the sharks gliding overhead.

'He's out with his girlfriend,' I lie.

'What's happening with this girl you've set your sights on?' he asks.

'Not a lot.'

'How come?'

'I keep trying to ask her out but the words just won't come.'

'Still?'

A raised eyebrow.

'Still.'

'Well, don't dither much longer, or you're going to watch her get snapped up all over again.' I watch the circling sharks. Suddenly they've all got the faces of lads in my year. I know Dad's right. But how do I do it? How? I've never actually made the opening move. Chloe went first, and so did Emma.

'I always mean to say it,' I tell him, 'but it just doesn't come out.'

'Then make it,' says Dad. 'Make it.'

He's about to say something else when he notices the girls heading for the gift shop.

'Yikes,' he says. 'Better intercept those two before they bankrupt me.'

I watch while he tries to explain why that gorgeous, cuddly shark, that cute 3-D seaworld diary, the adorable dolphin balloon and the unputdownable teddy bear purse are more than his bank account can bear. Standing there, negotiating limply, he's hardly setting an example of decisiveness, but so what? He's right about Julie. I have to say something. And soon. Before the sharks come any closer.

Tuesday 20th February
2.00 p.m.

Oh great. Bobby's waiting for me when Dad drops me off outside the house.

'You missed a good day, Bobby,' says Dad. 'Go somewhere nice with that girlfriend of yours?'

Bobby frowns.

'I haven't seen Emma today,' he says.

It's Dad's turn to frown. He looks at me but I turn away.

'Anyway,' says Dad, 'You can fend for yourself, Terry. I'm going to drop Katie off.'

Bobby and I watch him pull away.

'What was all that about?' asks Bobby.

'Beats me,' I say. 'You know what my dad's like.'

That seems to satisfy Bobby. But, as I open the front door, we slip right back into the discomfort zone.

'I challenged Emma about what Caitlin said.'

Heart sinking, toes curling, legs turning to jelly, spots before my eyes, rushing sound in my ears. It's a multi-sensory embarrassment experience.

'And?'

'She denied it. What do you expect?'

I seize on this like Leonardo Di Caprio clutching debris from the Titanic.

'Maybe Caitlin's making it up.'

'She's not like that,' says Bobby.

Leonardo slides senseless into the freezing Atlantic.

'If she was going to do something like that, why not months ago? No, Emma's got something to hide. I can tell.'

Why's this happening to me? I haven't done a thing to encourage her, but here I am feeling guilty as hell. I could lose my best mate . . . over nothing.

'Still planning to sort out whoever it is?' I ask.

'Too right,' says Bobby. 'What would you do?'

'Spend six months trying to pluck up the courage to say something, but what's that got to do with it?'

'I tell you,' Bobby says purposefully, 'no matter how long it takes, I'm going to track him down. If he was here right now I'd flatten him.'

He is here right now, and he's flat enough as it is.

Tuesday 20th February
4.00 p.m.

OK, so maybe this wasn't the cleverest thing to do, but I've called on Emma. I just had to clear the air. We're walking down Scotchbarn Lane, talking. Emma's wearing a black pencil skirt and a sleeveless top – in the middle of February! She's got goosebumps the size of golfballs. The price of looking good. For all my anxiety that Bobby might see us, I'm enjoying her company. She is one really cute girl. I've just finished telling her how upset Bobby is.

66

'Look Terry,' says Emma, 'You mean well, but I think I know how to handle Bobby.'

'But I've never seen him like this,' I say, interrupting. 'He's dead jealous. He's *never* jealous.'

'Good,' says Emma. 'Now he knows how I felt at New Year. It was a rotten thing to do.'

I agree. It was. But that isn't what I say.

'But Emma, you can't hold that against him forever!'

She stops and plants her hands stubbornly on her hips.

'Why not?'

For a few moments I can't think what to say. How would I feel in her place? In the end I manage a feeble:

'You just can't!'

'Terry, if you're going out with somebody, you don't kiss another girl, not right under your girlfriend's nose.'

'But this doesn't help,' I say. 'Too wrongs don't make a right.'

'Don't they?' says Emma. 'What's sauce for the goose is sauce for the gander.'

When we finally finish swopping idioms I say something she needs to know.

'He wants to know who the other guy is.'

'Well, I'm not telling him,' says Emma. 'And he's no right to ask after what he did. If he keeps going on about it, he'll lose me anyway.'

She's not telling him who she fancies. Well, that's something.

'I mean, I'm flattered,' I say. 'But this isn't going anywhere.'

Emma gives me a sideways look. She's got this weird expression on her face, like I've just started speaking Arabic.

'What isn't going anywhere? Terry, what *are* you on about?'

'You and me. The Valentine.'

Emma gives my cheek a friendly pinch.

'Oh, I get it now. *That's* why you're so excited. Oh Terry, you idiot.'

She laughs.

'There is no You and Me. I was flirting, that's all. I do it all the time. And I send lots of Valentine's. I even sent one to Six Guns, and Adrian McAllister.'

He's the fat kid in Mr Spottiswood's form. Half blimp, half doughnut.

'It's a laugh, that's all, a bit of a wind-up.'

Now I'm completely lost.

'So I've no need to worry?' I burble.

A reassuring shake of the head.

'I'm not the one . . . ?'

Emma mouths the word 'No' through smiling lips.

'Bobby's not going to . . . ?'

Emma gives me a playful hug. I feel every curve of her body and go hot all over.

'Poor Terry,' she says. 'No, you're not the one. And no, Bobby hasn't got any reason to fall out with you. Far from it, you're the best friend he could have.'

'Great,' I say.

But I don't feel great. I feel bewildered, totally and completely confused. I watch Emma walk past the swimming pool and turn right into St James Road. That's when a thought strikes me.

If not me, then who?

Tuesday 20th February
7.10 p.m.

I'm on my way home when I bump into Bobby.

'Where are you off to?' I ask.

I do it to give myself time to think of a reason why *I'm* here.

'Emma's,' says Bobby. 'What about you?'

For the first time, I see a glint of suspicion in his eyes. He's obviously never even considered me a candidate for the dirty, rotten scoundrel awards. Doesn't that make me feel good? I finally decide to do what I should have done all along. Tell him the whole truth. Now I know I'm not the one Emma's had the hots for, it's a lot easier. So that's what I do, I tell him: about the New Year's peck on the cheek, about the kiss outside the Sports Hall, about the Valentine's Day card. Then I take a deep breath and wait to hear what he has to say.

'You wally,' he says. 'Of course I didn't think it was you.'

'Good,' I say with a relieved smile, then a hurt: 'Hey, why not?'

'Because you're my mate, and mates don't do the dirty on each other.'

'Not because I'm an emaciated Chris Evans lookalike, then?'

'No.'

'Oh,' I say, 'that's all right then.'

'But it isn't all right, is it?' says Bobby, his face as long as one of Beckham's cross-field passes. 'There is somebody, isn't there?'

What can I say? Emma admitted as much not half an hour ago.

'Yes,' I say. 'You're right about that. There is somebody.'

'But who?' says Bobby, kicking a wall. 'Who?'

'I haven't got a clue,' I tell him. 'But I know one thing. You shouldn't go confronting her over it.'

'Why not?'

This is a bit rich. Me giving Bobby advice.

'She'll keep bringing up Pepsey Cooper. Why not just leave it for a bit?'

'Because,' says Bobby as he prepares to say words I never expected to hear from him, 'I love her.'

Tuesday 20th February
7.40 p.m.

In the end I left Bobby and Emma to it. Let's face it, there's nothing I can say that's going to make an ounce of difference. Besides, I had to get round to Dad's flat to listen to the match with him. He keeps promising to get On Digital, but he hasn't got round to it yet so it's United–Valencia at Old Trafford, live on Talk Radio.

'Cutting it fine, aren't you son?' says Dad.

'Bit of business,' I say.

'Girl business?'

'Kind of.'

'Good on you,' he says with a wink.

I don't tell him it isn't the girl he means. Instead I say:

'You sound brighter.'

'How do you mean?'

'You know, with the divorce going through.'

'Oh that. Well, you've got to move on, haven't you?'

The conversation is interrupted by a Ryan Giggs run, followed by a Killy Gonzalez counter-attack for Valencia.

'Close at both ends,' says Dad. 'It'd be nice to win this one. Get through to the quarter-finals with two games to spare.'

I nod but I can't help but think he's not as chirpy as he's trying to make out.

'Go on, Gary lad,' says Dad as Gary Neville goes on a run.

It's a good effort but it stays 0–0. No score. A bit like Julie and me. But hang on . . . wait just one minute . . . Cole . . . Andy Cole!

One–nil!

That's it, it doesn't have to be no score. I *can* talk to Julie. I *can* ask her out.

I will.

I'll do it.

Thanks United.

For returning the love.

As always.

Thursday 22nd February
2.45 p.m.

OK, so Wes Brown ended up scoring an own goal and Valencia got a 1–1 draw. It doesn't change a thing. United have spoken to me again, they've told me what I've got to do.

I've got to seize the opportunity, grasp the nettle, take the bull by the horns. Come to think of it, the way I feel I'd seize any opportunity, grasp anything, take any animal by the horns. You name it, I'd take it, grasp it, seize it. I'm reincarnated as Get Up And Go For It Man. *I will*, I'll go for it. No more Mr Wimp, no more being tongue-tied and trodden on. Nobody will ever take my dreams away from me. Never again. Nobody's going to walk all over me or kick sand in my face. Let the sharks circle, a new Terry Payne is born.

Except . . .

. . . every time I so much as think of asking Julie out there still seems to be an awful lot of the old Terry in me.

God, I'm a loser.

Oi you, Wimp – **No!** Get thee behind me, weak and snivelling fake Terry.

This is the real Terry, forged in the fire of lost love, steeled by the suffering of seeing her going out with Frisky Fitzy, made strong by a thousand slings and arrows. (That's right, we've just done *Hamlet* at school.)

You've got to tell her how you feel, Terry, and tell her now. But how?

And when?

I lie back on my bed, head resting on my laced fingers, and watch the rain streaming down the window pane.

That's the question, when?

What if the sharks move in? What if Julie goes out with one of them? I couldn't stand it happening again. I couldn't take the rejection a second time. No, I've got to act, and I've got to do it now.

But when? When can I see her?

'That's it!' I yell.

The gymnastics club, it's tonight. Saturdays, Tuesdays and **Thursdays**.

For a moment I think of phoning Bobby, asking him if he wants to play badminton. But I've done that before, last autumn. Julie can see straight through it. I just come over as a sad stalker. No, this time I'm going to be straight with her. I don't need anybody to hold my hand. I don't need any strategies and subterfuges. Just me and the girl and the God's honest truth.

Sounds good.

I just hope it works.

Thursday 22nd February
5.50 p.m.

I'm standing in the rain in the leisure centre car park. I've done this before, the night of the school dance, standing in the rain waiting for Julie. But that time I was a saddo. Now I'm reborn, a super-hero: Get Up And Go For It Man. So why are my legs turning to jelly? Why's my skin tickling and prickling? Why's there a lump the size of a dodo egg in my throat? Get Up And Go For It Man wouldn't behave like this. He'd be cool, steadfast and strong. He'd take the girl in his arms, look in her eyes and say . . .

Oh God, what *do* I say?

On the way over here I had it all worked out. Had it all prepared, I did, a speech, no, an *oration*. I should have written it down. No, you sad sack, you can't read something like this from a script! Maybe I should go. Yes, that's it, I'll sneak away under cover of darkness. Too late, there she is, getting out of a car. Come on, Terry, you can do this:

. . . cool . . .

. . . steadfast . . .

. . . strong.

Kelly sees me.

'Oh, look who's here, the Prescot Stalker.'

I want to dissolve, merge with the rain and trickle down the nearest drain, but I stand my ground.

'Hi Kelly,' I say, 'I want to talk to Julie. Privately, if you don't mind.'

What was that? Did you hear what I just said? I was cool, I was steadfast, I was strong. I am the strongest link. Hello!

Kelly and Julie exchange glances. To my amazement and absolute joy, Julie nods. Kelly walks reluctantly into the leisure centre foyer.

'Fire away, Terry,' says Julie. 'I'm listening.'

I look at her face, illuminated by the centre's floodlights. She's stunning, her long, black hair bound in skull plaits, her brown eyes looking into mine.

Ulp!

I've just forgotten how to talk!

'Terry?'

What do I do now?

I've never given it much thought until now, the ability to talk. It's natural, you dork. Well, it isn't natural now! I know it's got something to do with the jaws, the tongue, most of all the brain. But how do you engage them all at once? Suddenly the faculty of speech seems so far beyond me I could be a squid or a warthog.

What the hell do I do?

Then I remember, the prepared talk, the oration, all the things I've got to say, and it comes out in a stream of consciousness babble, a tumbling waterfall of words:

'Look Julie, you know I've always liked you. Always. Ever

since I saw you the first time at school. You were wearing blue. I know, I know, it doesn't really matter what you were wearing. Well, it does of course. I'm not implying I've thought of you wearing nothing . . .'

Aaaargghh! What am I saying? My mouth's just been invaded by aliens from the Planet Gobbledygook. They're making me come out with complete gibberish! Quick, focus. Cool, steadfast, strong.

'No, what I mean is, I was gutted when you went out with Fitz. I just couldn't find the words to ask you out myself, but I like you Julie. I really like you. I know you probably think I'm a complete and utter loser, and I'm only in the top set for English and French and I bet you think they don't count, and I'm a Man U fan and you support Liverpool, but crazier things have happened.'

Name one? asks a secret voice inside my brain. But I'm not about to be sidetracked. I've been waiting for this moment for seven lousy months and, no matter what it takes, I'm going to say what I feel. That way, at least I've gone down fighting.

'There's never been anyone but you, Julie. I know I went out with Chloe for a bit, but that's because you were with Fitz. And she asked me when I was down, when I was *vulnerable*. It just kind of happened, but I ended it. She wasn't you. She just wasn't you. And Emma, you got that all wrong. I'd never mess around with her. All you saw was a friendly peck on the cheek. She's Bobby's girl.'

Isn't that a pop song? the secret voice asks, something I've heard round Dad's flat. *I wanna be, duh duh, Bobby's girl*. Who was it, Cilla Black, Dusty Springfield? Dad would know. Shut up! Shut up! There's a nerd in my brain. Get out of my head, will you? I take a deep breath.

'There's one last thing, I didn't break Fitz's ankle on purpose. He went for me first. I know you don't want to listen, but it's the truth. It really is.'

She's staring at me, eyes wide and with no discernible expression on her face. My eyes flick away for a second and I see her legs. They're shapely and they look tanned. She's wearing shorts. She's fantastic. Stop it, Terry. Focus. What's she thinking? I try to replay the speech to myself and it comes out as complete gibberish. Oh God, she thinks I'm mad. I'm the

Mad Manc and I'm ogling her legs. I force my eyes away from her legs and back to her face and I make my last bid for happiness.

'Look, you probably think I'm a complete loony toon by now, but it's just because . . .'

Deep breath. Here goes nothing, just my whole life.

' . . . I like you so much. Will you go out with me?'

Would *you*? asks the secret voice.

Of course I would, I'd take pity on a nice guy – even if he's dumb as a mule and crazy as a coot – and I'd say yes. But I'm not Julie. She's already told me she doesn't want to rush into another relationship right away. What's she going to say? It's going to be no. I just know it.

For the next split-second time stands still. The rain stops falling, the car tyres stop hissing on the rain-drenched streets, the trees bend their heads to listen, and Julie says:

'OK.'

OK! O for Omigod, K for Kerrumbs.

That's it, OK? All that yearning and wishing and hoping and she just comes out with it like that?

OK!

'Look Terry,' she says, her words barely audible over my erratic heartbeat. 'I've got to go inside now. We're preparing for a big display and I can't be late. Call me after ten o'clock. We'll arrange something.'

'Ten o'clock,' I say. 'Is that when you finish?'

'No, it's when the Liverpool–Roma coverage finishes on telly. I'll be home in time for the second half.'

Without another word, she puts her bags down, slips her arms round my neck and kisses me full on the lips. The kiss burns through me like a brand, scalding me with joy and relief.

She said yes. The most beautiful girl in the world just said yes!

I notice that she's standing on tiptoes to kiss me. I don't believe it. I've always thought she was taller than me, but she isn't. I just felt that way, a case of The Beauty and The Dwarf.

'You won't forget to ring me, will you?' she says, pulling away.

'I'd forget to breathe first,' I say and she giggles.

I'm stunned. I've actually said something half-way roman-

74

tic. I watch her run up the steps. By the door she turns round and waves. Even after she's gone I carry on standing and watching, imagining her there by the door.

Returning the love.

PART TWO

With the Girl
or
Theatre of
Dreams

1

You won't believe the movie Julie wanted to see. 'What Women Want', it was called. Like I've got the foggiest idea! But I'd better cotton on quick. All these months I've sort of thought that history ended once the girl said yes, I'll go out with you. Then you just had to settle down for the Happy Ever Afters. What was I thinking of? This is where the difficult stuff really begins. I'm not going out with a dream of Julie, I'm going out with Julie. Maybe she's feeling the same way, wondering what the real Terry Payne is like. We're walking in the rain, dodging the cars as they head for the main road, when Julie slips her arm through mine.

'Walk me to the bus stop?' she says.

'I'd walk you all the way back to Huyton,' I tell her.

'The bus stop will do,' she says, laughing.

I remember the time I saw her at the same bus stop with Fitz. My skin catches fire at the thought. But I've got to be strong. Don't mention him. Don't act jealous. I'm on strict orders from Dad and Bobby. Cool is good, obsessive is bad. Each of them in their own way has been coaching me on being with The Girl.

'This is great,' I say. 'Being with you. Can I see you again tomorrow?'

'Sorry,' says Julie. 'I can't.'

'Oh.'

It's a big, disappointed *oh*, as heavy as a stone. She stops and turns my face towards her with fingers chilled by the night rain.

'Hey, I've really enjoyed this evening,' she says. 'You're not like Fitz. I don't have to fend you off.'

I remember Fitz's reputation. Somebody, Caitlin I think, once described him as a sex-mad octopus. A bit too graphic a description for my liking.

'I'm not turning you down,' says Julie. 'I won't be in Liverpool, that's all.'

'Where will you be?'

'Cardiff, of course. The Worthington Cup Final.'

'You mean you're going?'

It must have been a dream when Julie ceremonially burned her Liverpool scarf and became a Man U fan.

'We all are. Me, Mum, Dad, my brothers. Terry, this is Liverpool v Birmingham, our best chance of silverware for years.'

I call her brothers Huey, Duey and Louie. Julie calls them Gerard, Josh and John-Joe, probably because those are their real names.

'We're going on a coach and staying overnight in a hotel in Cardiff. One of the parents in the gymnastics club arranged it.'

'You're not telling me your family can fill a whole coach?'

'Of course not, there's a crowd of us.'

'Do I know anybody?'

'One or two,' says Julie.

Her voice falters slightly.

'Such as?'

'Kelly, of course. Gary, Paul, Pepsy, Jamie . . .'

She takes a little breath despite herself.

' . . . and Fitz.'

Remember what Dad and Bobby said, don't get jealous. Jealousy is the ultimate turn-off for a girl.

'Oh.'

Yipes! That sounded pretty jealous.

'You're not going to make a fuss, are you?'

Me, make a fuss about her going away to Wales with her ex? Of course not.

'No.'

I try to sound breezy and careless, but it comes out about as breezy and careless as an Eminem song. Julie stands on her tiptoes and kisses me. It's everything I've heard about in a kiss. Chloe's kisses were nice but they never made me feel this way. Julie's lips press firmly against mine. Her mouth opens just the slightest bit and she gives a little sigh. My skin tingles, my stomach fills with butterflies, heat floods through me. I feel like I'm floating up towards the stars. But, as she pulls away, there's this nagging doubt at the back of my mind. I've done this. I used to kiss Chloe this way when she started asking too many questions. It's the ultimate tactical shut up.

'You've nothing to worry about with Fitz, you know,' says Julie, squeezing my upper arms.

'Of course not,' I say, struggling not to pout, not to be jealous. 'You just went out with him for seven months.'

'And I would have gone out with you if you'd only asked.'

'Really?'

'Of course, really. You should have seen how many times I put Fitz off. But you never said a word.'

If I could kick my own backside, I'd be doing it now.

'I saw you looking at me.'

'You did?'

So much for those discreet looks of mine.

'Why didn't you say something?'

'I was . . . Oh, this sounds stupid.'

Julie is looking at me with this amused expression on her face.

'Go on, what?'

'I was shy. You're so . . . you know. And I'm so . . .'

'Well,' says Julie, throwing her head back and laughing that rich, strong laugh of hers, 'that explains everything.'

She's teasing me, but I don't care. Julie teases the way most people caress: softly, gently, beautifully.

'You're lovely,' I say, still trying to explain. 'You're good at sport, you're popular, you're in the top set at everything, all the boys are after you . . .'

'Are they?'

'Are you kidding?'

'I thought it was Kelly,' says Julie.

'No way,' I say. 'Have you seen you?'

'Watch *Friends* a lot, do you?' asks Julie. 'That's a Monica line.'

'Figures,' I say, 'I have to steal stuff off other people. I've never been able to express myself.'

Julie kisses me again, pressing her body up against me. I don't want this evening to end.

'Terry, you're doing just fine.'

All my *Friends* watching kicks in again and I say:

'Oh . . .'
. . . my . . .
. . . God!'

Saturday 24th February
2.00 p.m.

I've been in more embarrassing situations, but I can't really remember when. I've come down to see Julie off. She doesn't mind. She says it's *sweet*. Everybody else seems to mind, though.

Kelly said: 'I don't know what you see in him. Loser.'

Fitz said (on the quiet, when Julie wasn't around): 'Think you're so clever, don't you, nicking my girl. Well, don't get too comfortable, MnM, I'm not finished, not by a long chalk. I'm nearly ready to play again. I'll have you, Manc.'

Gerard, Josh and John-Joe said, (one after the other and independently of each other): 'I thought our Julie had better taste. A Mad Manc!'

Gary said (to Fitz, but for my benefit): 'Watch he doesn't kick you again.'

So it's a relief when Julie takes me by the hand and leads me round the corner where nobody can see us, and says: 'Kiss me. This has got to last me the weekend.'

I'm just planning my Kiss that Will Last the Weekend when Julie takes the initiative and I feel the warmth of her lips on mine. No matter how much I try not to listen, I find myself haunted by the secret voice saying: I wonder if she kissed Fitz like this? There's no point my saying anything like that to Julie so I kiss her back hotly, running my fingers through the cascade of raven black hair, then squeezing her back, letting my hands slide down to her hips.

'Have a good weekend,' says Julie.

What, on my own in Prescot!

'Yes, you too,' I say, without that much conviction.

It's not only because Man U fans find it hard to wish Liverpool well, but because I can't get Fitz's face out of my mind. Julie might say it's over. I'm not so sure he thinks so.

'I'll phone you from Cardiff,' she says, jogging towards the coach.

'Have you got my number?' I ask, as she jumps on board.

'Both of them,' says Julie. 'Home and mobile. Your mum gave them to me.'

Mum, have I ever told you I love you?

'Don't forget,' I say.

'I won't,' says Julie.

As the coach pulls away she blows me a kiss. And it isn't sarcastic or anything. It's for real. As for Fitz, he gives me a two-finger salute, and it's not because he thinks he's Winston Churchill!

Saturday 24th February
4.30 p.m.

Alex Nyarko has just been sent off so Everton are down to ten men against Ipswich. Bobby starts kicking seven bells out of my bedside cabinet. The alarm clock falls to the floor and starts to bleat pitifully.

'Hey, go and kick your own furniture!'

'That was a nothing challenge,' says Bobby. 'Do these stupid refs want us to go down?'

I don't know how he can be so sure it was a nothing challenge. We're listening to the game on the radio! United don't play until tomorrow.

'Do you know how many players this ref's sent off this season?' rants Bobby. 'Seven!'

Something tells me this isn't just about Everton's prospects of survival. The uncertainty over Emma is getting him down.

'Have you had another argument with Emma?' I ask.

Bobby nods.

'She won't tell me who she's been seeing.'

'Why, did you think she would?'

'She says it was nothing, just a way of getting even with me for New Year, so I should drop it.'

'Maybe you should.'

'That's a bit rich,' says Bobby, 'coming from somebody who's going mad about his girlfriend being in Cardiff with Fitz.'

'Who's going mad?'

'Well, you're not happy.'

He's right. I'm not. I just know everybody will be trying to poison her against me. Especially Fitz.

'She isn't there with Fitz,' I retort. 'She's with a load of people.'

'Yes, including Fitz.'

Just then Everton go 1–0 down. Serves Bobby right for bringing up Cardiff!

He punches the bedside cabinet.

'What *have* you got against my furniture?' I ask, protecting the alarm clock from further punishment.

Bobby shrugs, and immediately Everton go 2–0 down.

'Look at that,' he groans. 'One minute we're coasting to a 0–0 draw, the next the ref sends Nyarko off and we're losing 2–0.'

'So are you going to drop it?' I ask, meaning him and the Who's Emma Been Seeing? investigation.

'Would you?' he asks pointedly.

No, I think.

'Of course,' I say.

Saturday 24th February
10.00 p.m.

She hasn't phoned.

Here am I sitting waiting for *Match of the Day* and Julie's out having fun with all her mates . . . and Fitz.

'I'm making a coffee,' says Mum. 'Do you want anything?'

I shake my head. I'm too miserable to eat. There's snow on the ground outside. I hope United have got the underground heating on. I need a good win against Arsenal to lift my spirits.

Fitz! Why did he have to be born?

'Sure?' asks Mum. 'I bought biscuits.'

'No thanks.'

'I'll have a biscuit,' shouts Amy from upstairs.

'No, you won't, young lady. Now lights out and go to sleep.'

'Why does Terry get a biscuit?'

'He's seven years older.'

'That's not fair!'

'Who said life was fair? Now go to sleep.'

The phone goes and I bolt for it. It's only Dad asking whether I'm going round for the match tomorrow.

Of course I am, I tell him.

'How was the big date?'

'Great.'

I'm being monosyllabic so he will get off the phone. What if Julie is ringing me right now?

'I'll see you tomorrow then.'

'Yes, goodnight Dad.'

'Waiting for Julie to phone?' asks Mum.

'Does it show?'

'Oh yes.'

She sits down. She's got a coffee but no biscuits.

'You're very disciplined,' I observe.

'It's seeing the weight come off,' she says. 'Gives me the encouragement to give the biccies a miss.'

I nod absent-mindedly.

'Don't take it too much to heart if she can't ring you,' says Mum. 'She's with all her family and friends.'

'I know,' I say.

But it isn't what I want to hear. If I mean anything to her, if she cares, then she'll phone.

Saturday 24th February
10.45 p.m.

She still hasn't phoned.

I never thought I would say this, but I can't keep my mind on *Match of the Day*. Come to think of it, I don't even know which game I'm watching. There's only one thing on my mind.

Where is she? Why hasn't she rung?

'Sure you don't want a biscuit?' asks Mum. 'Hobnob?'

I smile. It always used to be me comforting her with Hobnobs.

'Go on then.'

I think they call it comfort eating. I'm on my fourth biscuit when the phone rings.

'Terry?'

'Julie!'

Except it comes out Zurrbleee on account of the Hobnob. Crumbs pebble-dash the phone table.

'What's the matter with your voice?'

'Hobnob.'

'I beg your pardon?'

'I was eating a biscuit.'

'Oh. Are you missing me?'

'Loads.'

I almost tell her I couldn't eat, but the Hobnob is making a liar out of me.

'I thought . . .'

No, not the guilt trip. Not attractive to a woman. Note 3 from Dad's Compendium of Advice on Females. I keep shtum, but Julie rumbles me.

' . . . That I wouldn't phone? Hey you, Reliable's my middle name.'

And Jealous is mine.

'We've been out for a meal.'

'Yes, who's "we"?'

'Just the family . . . and Kelly.'

Oh joy! No Fitz.

'Nobody else?'

Stupid. That is definitely jealousy. Let's hope she hasn't noticed.

'Fitz went out with his mates,' says Julie pointedly.

She's teasing in that gentle way of hers.

'Anyway, here's wishing you really bad luck for the game against Arsenal,' she says.

'Yes, same for you against Birmingham,' I reply. 'I hope you get hammered.'

'Up the Gunners!' says Julie.

'Come on you Brummies,' I answer.

We both laugh. I never thought I'd be able to laugh about football!

'See you in school on Monday,' says Julie.

'Yes, see you then.'

I'm wondering whether it's too soon or too corny – or just too damned pathetic – to say 'I love you' when she hangs up.

Because I definitely do.

Sunday 25th February
12.50 p.m.

I'm so nervous I can hardly stand.

For starters, there's the match: United v Arsenal. First and second in the Premiership. If they win then, maybe, just maybe, they stand a chance of catching us. The gap would be down to ten points. So if we lost at Leeds and Liverpool . . . I start doing the maths . . . then went down at Spurs . . . More maths. I might not be in the top set, but I can tot up the League table. And lost to City . . . Oh crumbs, our monster lead doesn't seem quite so impregnable when you put it like that. The Gunners did it once before. Overmars scored the winner at Old Trafford and stood all cocky and superior after beating Gary Neville and Peter Schmeichel. After that, Dad and I hated all things Dutch, except for Jaap Stam, of course. We wouldn't let Mum buy Edam cheese and we wouldn't allow a tulip in the house! Arsenal went on to win the League and Cup double. It was a lousy summer that year. The signs aren't good for a midday showdown. Andy Cole and Ryan Giggs are unavailable. I've got a bad feeling about this.

Then there's Julie and me. Don't get me wrong. Everything seems to be going fine. Better than fine, we're talking Walk on Air Wondiferous. I can smell her hair just thinking of her.

She's so open and sweet and affectionate. Boy, is she affectionate! You wouldn't think she was the most gorgeous girl in the whole school. She could pick anybody and she's going out with me.

Me!

Which is half the problem, really. I mean, what on earth does she see in me? If I was a girl, I wouldn't go out with me. Too shy, too skinny, too ginger, too . . . too . . . TOO TERRY PAYNE! Put me next to Fitz and there's just no competition. He's all muscly and mesomorphic, he's sickeningly clever and everybody thinks he's Mr Wonderful. Most of all he's down there in Cardiff with her. What's to stop him rekindling the flame? Not me, that's for sure.

I can hardly stand.

So I sit down.

Heavily.

'Hey,' says Dad, 'watch the chair. The springs aren't too good.'

'Sorry.'

'So how's Julie?'

'In Cardiff.'

'Oh dear, missing her, are you?'

'There's more to it than that. Fitz is down there at the Cup Final.'

'Fitz?'

'Her ex. I told you.'

'Sorry. Head like a sieve. Still, I wouldn't worry. She dumped him, didn't she?'

'Yes, but . . .'

'But what?'

'I'm a loser.'

Dad's eyes flash with anger.

'Now you can cut that out. I'm the world's expert at feeling sorry for myself and I tell you, Terry, it gets you nowhere. If she's decided to go out with you, then you must have something going for you.'

I look up hopefully.

'You reckon?'

'Definitely.'

Sunday 25th February
1.02 and 47 seconds.

I've got something going for me, all right. Dwight Yorke has scored. A Paul Scholes step-over, a one-two with Dwight and I'm in seventh heaven.

Sunday 25th February
1.15 and 26 seconds.

No-o-o-o-o-o-o-o . . .

  o-o-o-o-o-o-o-o-o-o-o-o . . .

  o-o-o-o-o-o-o-o-o-o-o-o-o-o-o!!!!

Arsenal have equalised. Thierry Henry. That's it, chuck out the garlic. I hate everything French, except Mickael Silvestre and Fabien Barthez, of course.

Sunday 25th February
1.17 and 10 seconds.

Ye-e-e-e-e-e . . .
  e-e-e-e-e-e-e-e . . .
  e-e-e-e-e-e-e-e-e-e-e-s-s-s-s-s!!!!!
Seventh heaven again! Two for Dwight Yorke.

Sunday 25th February
1.22 and 30 seconds.

A-a-a-a-a-a-a- . . .

Sunday 25th February
1.22 and 40 seconds.

O-o-o-o-oo-o-o-o- . . .
  Wah-hooooooo!!!
  It's a Dwight Yorke hat-trick.
  Is there an eighth heaven?

Sunday 25th February
1.24 and 15 seconds.

Un . . .
  be . . .
    liev . . .
      a . . .
        ble!
Roy Keane makes it four.
  I'm in ninth heaven, and Andy Gray sums it up: 'Arsenal are
on the end of a spanking.'

Sunday 25th February
1.37 and 46 seconds.

Now it's five – let me repeat that – five goals to one.
  Ole Gunner Solskjaer, the baby-faced assassin.

Sunday 25th February
2.45 p.m.

Terry to universe, Terry to universe, I have just witnessed Big Bang Two. Manchester United Six, Arsenal one!

Ready, Teddy Sheringham.

It's the twenty-second time in the history of the Premiership that United have scored five or more goals in a game, and we've never handed out a more satisfying thrashing.

'Happy now?' asks Dad.

Oh yes.

Sunday 25th February
5.00 p.m.

By the way, Liverpool have won the Worthington Cup.

Sunday 25th February
8.00 p.m.

The phone goes. It's Julie. It's a bit different to the last call. There's loads of shouting in the background.

'Where are you?' I ask.

'Motorway services. Did you see it?'

'Yes, 6–1.'

'Not United, Terry, *Liverpool*.'

Terry Payne's match report. Birmingham should have won. They were robbed. A blatant penalty turned down in extra time. I don't say that, of course. This *is* the girl I love.

'Yes, you did OK.'

'OK? We won the Cup!'

There's a noise like a rhino breaking wind.

'What's that?'

'Fitz.'

That flatulent rhino.

'Oh.'

It's my lead balloon *Oh* again.

'Go away!'

Julie's talking to somebody next to her. She is obviously trying to hang on to her mobile.

'I said, clear off!'

'Julie?'

'It's OK, Terry. They're excited, that's all.'

Oh, Fitz will be excited all right, excited about you, Julie!

I hear something like a door slamming.

'Terry, can you hear me?'

'Yes.'

'I'm in the ladies' loo. Nobody can get to me in here.'

A lavatory never sounded so romantic! For a moment I wonder whether to say the three little words. I'm dying to, but I don't want to be premature, or off-putting, or stupid. I've asked Dad and Bobby what they think. When do I say *I love you*?

Dad: When you're sure she's the one.

Bobby: Never.

I'm sure she's the one, but in the end I don't manage anything better than:

'Have you had a good time?'

'Oh Terry, it's been fantastic.'

But what, what *exactly* has been fantastic?

'I'll tell you all about it in school tomorrow. I got you a present.'

She's got *me* a present. That isn't right. I should be buying her presents.

'Julie, you shouldn't.'

'Yes, I should. I definitely should. Anyway, got to go. I'm running out of talk time.'

'Bye Julie.'

Maybe I should just say it. Go on, what harm will it do? Three little words. What's so hard about that? I open my mouth but as I form the words the phone goes dead. We're out of time.

2

This must be the best week of my life. It started when Julie
gave me this naff cuddly red dragon she brought back from
Cardiff. But so what if it was naff? It was from her, the first
present between us. I've got it hanging over my bed.

Bobby was disgusted when he saw it: 'You going soft on
me?' he asked.

'Definitely,' I told him.

Julie was made up when she saw it. I think she had a
sneaking suspicion I would chuck it in the bin. I think putting
it on display like that has kind of convinced her I'm in touch
with my female side.

We've been inseparable all week. I think Kelly is feeling
really put out by it all. Tonight, we're baby-sitting Amy
together. Mum's gone to her jogging club. Julie and I are
sitting on the couch. Amy is curled up in the armchair across
the room. She gets to stay up until ten o'clock every Friday
night. It's a vampire-lovers' double bill on Sky One: *Buffy, the
Vampire Slayer* followed by *Angel*.

'Shouldn't Mum be home?' asks Amy.

I glance at the wall clock.

'She's only five minutes late,' I tell her. 'Nothing to worry
about.'

Just then the phone rings. It's Mum.

'Hi Terry, is it OK if I go for a drink with some of the
members?'

Some of the members? Somehow that doesn't ring quite true.

'I was going to walk Julie to the bus stop,' I say.

'What time is she going?'

'We have to leave the house at half past ten.'

'I'll be home by then,' says Mum. 'And if I'm not, I'll run her home.'

'Fair enough.'

I hear a man's voice in the background.

'Who's that?'

'Oh, just one of the members.'

That again, *one of the members*. She's definitely up to something.

'That was Mum,' I tell Amy.

It's the adverts.

'Anybody want a snack?' I ask.

'Can I have Cheerios in here?' asks Amy.

It's one of Mum's rules. No breakfast cereal in the living room. I've spilt mine down the couch twice. She went mad.

'Yes,' I say. 'So long as you sit on a cushion on the floor.'

Amy goes wide-eyed with surprise.

'I like you going out with Julie,' she says. 'You act nice when she's around.'

I glance at a smiling Julie. She's definitely good for me. She's even got me doing some maths revision.

'Yes, I suppose I do.'

Julie follows me into the kitchen. It's the first time we've been out of Amy's sight. While I pour out the cereal Julie slips her arms round my waist and squeezes gently. I stroke her forearms. God, this feels good, like we're a proper couple.

'Mum should be back for half past ten,' I tell her. 'She'll run you home if she's any later.'

'No problem,' says Julie. 'What's she doing anyway?'

'She's gone out with some of the members of the jogging club.'

'Sounds like a feller to me,' Julie observes.

'That,' I murmur, wondering what Dad would say, 'is exactly what I thought.'

Friday 2nd March
10.35 p.m.

We're at the bus stop, having a cuddle while we wait. There are four other people waiting. They've all got their backs to us.

Funny that, how people don't like watching you when you're getting all lovey-dovey.

'Your mum looked a bit flustered,' says Julie. 'It's definitely a feller.'

'You think so?'

'Terry, I know so.'

I've got this mental picture of a tall, lean man in jogging bottoms and a London Marathon T-shirt. Mum with a boyfriend. Weird!

'I saw you here with Fitz once,' I say.

Julie stiffens.

'When?'

'Months ago. I was over there watching.'

Julie looks up at me.

'Did you follow us?'

I remember Kelly's stalker jibes and shake my head quickly.

'Of course not. I was on my way home, that's all. Fitz was trying it on.'

Julie laughs.

'He was *always* trying it on!'

My face must be giving me away because Julie immediately says:

'Oh, don't go all jealous on me, Terry. I made sure he behaved himself.'

'I try not to be jealous,' I say. 'It's just . . .'

'What?'

'He's so good at everything.'

'Don't put yourself down, Terry. You're worth two of Fitz.'

'So how come you still hang round with him?'

Julie frowns, obviously frustrated with me.

'Terry, he's a mate.'

'Are you going to the match together?'

'Well, not tomorrow. We're away at Leicester. The next home game we will be, but there's a gang of us: me, Kelly, Gary. My dad and our Gerard go as well. It's not like it's just the two of us. You can't want me to stop seeing my friends.'

I wish I could! I confine myself to a lukewarm, 'no, of course not.'

'Because I'm with you now, Terry. One hundred per cent.'

We kiss to seal the bargain.

'Anyway,' says Julie, 'here's my bus.'

I'm watching her climb on board when this old dear smiles at me.

'She's a lovely girl, son. You hang on to her.'

I smile back. I just hope I can.

Saturday 3rd March
12.10 p.m.

'Seen this girl of yours?' asks Dad.

'Not today. She's gone to her gymnastics club, then she's going into town shopping.'

'Ninety-three per cent,' murmurs Bobby, who has been conspicuous by his silence.

'What?'

'Ninety-three per cent. The number of teenage girls who say that store-hopping is their favourite activity.'

'Oh.'

The three of us are watching Leeds–Man U on Dad's TV. It's a tight game with few chances. At half-time Dad makes some butties.

'Your mum OK?' asks Dad.

I must have hesitated.

'Terry?'

May as well be honest, I tell myself.

'I think she's seeing someone.'

Dad looks at the plate of sandwiches for a moment, then recovers himself and shrugs.

'She's a free woman now. She can do what she wants.'

I lead the way into the living-room, but not before I let him know I'm not fooled:

'Now say it like you mean it.'

United look like they are going to hang on to an undeserved 1–1 draw until Wes Brown turns a cross into his own net.

'Oh no!'

But the linesman saves our bacon. It's ruled offside.

'Lucky,' says Bobby. 'Very lucky.'

This time he meets our disapproving glare.

'Well, I've got the right to my opinion, haven't I?'
In unison, Dad and I roar 'No!'

Saturday 3rd March
4.15 p.m.

I'm following Bobby out of the door when I lean across to Dad.

'Are you OK?' I ask. 'About Mum?'

'It's a matter of having to be,' he says.

I leave it at that and catch Bobby up.

'You're in a funny mood today,' I say. 'Something happened with Emma?'

'She says either I stop interrogating her about this other lad, or we're finished.'

'So why not drop it?' I ask. 'She isn't seeing him any more, is she?'

Bobby frowns.

'I don't think so.'

'Then leave it, Bob. You're driving her away.'

'It's hard,' he says. 'I just can't get it out of my mind. Who do you think it is?'

This is becoming an obsession with him.

'Bobby, I've no idea.'

'No, of course you haven't,' says Bobby, with a touch of dark humour. 'I mean, you thought it was you, didn't you?'

I shrug.

'We all make mistakes.'

'Are you seeing Julie tonight?' Bobby asks.

I nod.

'What are you doing?'

'You're not going to believe this.'

'Go on, try me.'

'I'm going to her house for tea.'

'Are you nuts! They're all mad Liverpudlians. What are you going for?'

'Julie wants me to.'

'Mum, Dad, three brothers, all Kop-ites. They'll eat you alive.'

'It can't be that bad,' I say.

'You sure about that?'

96

Actually no.

Gulp!

Saturday 3rd March
5.20 p.m.

I've been wandering around for ten minutes. Julie said get there at 5.30, and I don't want to arrive too early. But something changes my mind. A couple of lads start sizing me up. I don't like the look of them. Ten minutes isn't *too* early, I decide. I make a move. The two lads follow me for a while then lose interest. I wonder if they can smell Mancunian – even an adopted Manc like me. I find Julie's house. Double glazing, hanging basket, new car outside. The family doesn't seem badly off. I ring the doorbell and wait, confidence draining out of me. I hope Julie answers. I see somebody in the frosted glass. It isn't her. When the door opens I find myself looking at a tall, gangly thirteen year old. This must be Huey, I mean Gerard. Duey and Louie will be lurking inside, plotting the downfall of the Mad Manc.

'Hi,' I say, as brightly as I can manage.

'Ju,' he shouts, ignoring me, 'It's your Manc.'

Julie shoves past, swatting him with a copy of the *Echo*, and waves me in.

'Ignore him, Terry. Come in.'

I follow her. I find myself thinking about condemned men and their final walk. I glimpse a long Ikea table set for seven people. Julie leads me past the kitchen and into the living-room.

'Terry, this is my mum.'

Dad once told me that, if you wanted to know whether to settle down with a girl, take a look at her mother. That's what she'll be like in a few years. So I take a look. Mrs Carter is tall, slim and tanned-looking. More than Julie, even. She has oval brown eyes and a full mouth. She passes the acceptable mother test.

'This is my dad.'

'Alright there, Terry,' says the thick-set, middle-aged man in a strong Scouse accent. 'Lucky this morning, weren't you?'

'A draw was a fair result,' I say defensively.

I keep quiet about Liverpool going down 2–0. Bad etiquette to gloat, I reckon.

'This is Josh,' Julie says.

Gerard's smaller version ignores me.

'And this is John-Joe.'

He ignores me too. Julie rolls her eyes.

'I hope you like Italian,' says Mr Carter.

'Love it,' I say.

'Good, because my wife's Italian.'

I glance at a smiling Mrs Carter. I suppose that explains Julie's bronzed skin, though you'd think it would have been bleached a bit by the Merseyside drizzle.

'We play your lot on the thirty-first, don't we?' says Mr Carter.

'Yes, that's right.'

'We'll get the double over you this year,' says Josh.

'Batter you,' says John-Joe.

I glance at Julie. What do I say? I decide not to rise to it.

'We'll see,' I say. 'Should be a good game.'

As if I care whether it's a good game. I want us to win, that's all!

'Well,' says Mr Carter, 'Shall we eat?'

I follow them, hoping I get to sit next to Julie. John-Joe steals my place. On purpose, I think.

'Hey you,' says Julie. 'Shift!'

'Why, want to sit next to lover boy, do you?' sneers Gerard.

'Now stop teasing,' says Mrs Carter.

She sounds pretty Scouse for an Italian.

I eventually get to sit next to Julie.

'Do you like spaghetti carbonara?' asks Mrs Carter.

'Probably,' I say.

Julie and her parents laugh, the three boys scowl. I spend the next ten minutes trying not to trail spaghetti against my shirt. It isn't easy. The food is lovely, though. I've been living on microwave meals since Dad left. Mum's always in a rush. I complete the meal with only two minor food streaks, and they match my top so it doesn't really matter. Thank goodness it wasn't bolognese. Mr Carter asks me about school. The conversation turns to the football team.

'I hear you're quite useful,' he says.

I glance at Julie and smile.

'Useful at breaking people's legs,' snorts Gerard.

Julie glares at him.

'Terry says it was a fifty-fifty ball.'

I look at her. She believes me!

'Besides,' says Julie, 'these things happen.'

Or maybe she half-believes me.

'It's a hard game.'

Or maybe she doesn't believe me at all!

'I'm afraid my three boys are secretary, treasurer and president of the Fitz Fan Club,' says Mr Carter.

Now that's a name I didn't want to hear over tea. I bet Fitz could eat spaghetti Doo-Dah without smearing it all over his shirt. To reassure me, Julie squeezes my leg under the table. I prickle with pleasure.

'Yes,' I say ruefully. 'He's dead popular.'

Saturday 3rd March
7.00 p.m.

We're going bowling. I'm glad to get out of the house. Huey, Duey and Louie have been hard work all evening, always trying to make me look like an idiot. And they dropped something into the conversation that's got me really worried.

'That wasn't too bad, was it Terry?' asks Julie as the bus pulls away from the stop.

'No,' I say, 'It wasn't *too* bad.'

'Go on,' says Julie in that long-suffering way of hers. 'What's bothering you now?'

'What did Gerard mean?' I ask. 'He said something about Easter. Just after we'd eaten. You and Fitz and Easter.'

'Oh, take no notice of our Ged.'

'But what did he mean?'

Julie gives that little sigh of hers, like a mum having to explain to a little kid why the windows steam up in cold weather, or where babies come from, or why the cat couldn't get up again after it got run over.

'I'm in the gymnastics club, right?'

'Yes.'

'And Hayley Fitzpatrick is in the same club.'

99

'Yes.'

I don't like where this is heading. I've seen Fitz at the leisure centre picking his kid sister up, so it isn't exactly news to me.

'And you know we do displays in different parts of the country?'

'Of course. You've got that Ministrada thing next weekend.'

'Right. Well, not only do gym clubs from all over the country come to Liverpool. We go to them too. And at Easter we go to Edinburgh for the next competition.'

It rings a bell. They all went to the Isle of Man last year.

'And . . . ?'

'And,' says Julie, starting to look uncomfortable. 'Hayley's whole family goes to support her.'

'Including Fitz,' I say.

'Yes,' says Julie. 'Including Fitz. His parents don't feel they can leave him alone in the house. I don't blame them really, he is a bit wild.'

While I'm wondering just how wild he got with her, Julie continues.

'Oh Terry, I wish you'd stop worrying about him. It's over. To be honest, it's basically been over for months. I just couldn't bring myself to tell him.'

She takes my left hand between hers.

'Listen, if this is going to work you've got to trust me. Half the reason I broke up with Fitz was because he was so jealous.'

'What was he jealous of?'

Julie chuckles.

'Why, you of course.'

'Me!'

Now this is starting to get interesting.

'Yes, didn't you know?'

'Of course not. What's he got to be jealous of? I don't get it.'

'Every time he saw us talking he would go mad. He's very insecure that way.'

Fitz insecure! Now I've heard everything.

'So are you OK about Edinburgh?'

'Yes,' I say. 'Of course I am.'

I sit there looking OK about Edinburgh. I look out at the street lights snaking into the distance. I think I pulled it off pretty well. But OK about them being in Scotland together? I wish.

Saturday 3rd March
7.35 p.m.

'See anybody we know?' says Julie, when we get to the bowling alley.

She means anybody *she* knows. Mr Popular I'm not.

'Not yet,' I grunt.

It's not like I'm trying very hard. I just want it to be Julie and me. I mean – Kelly, Gary, Paul, Pepsey, Jamie, my ex Chloe, I don't fancy hanging round with them all night. They're all members of the Fitz fan club.

'Hang on,' says Julie. 'That's Pepsey, isn't it?'

She leads the way. It's Pepsey Cooper all right. I can't help picturing her crying at the New Year's party after Paul caught her snogging Bobby. That certainly knocked the fizz out of her!

'Hi Pepsey, anybody around?'

The moment she lays eyes on us Pepsey's face goes as white as a sheet.

'Where's Paul?' Julie asks, looking round. There are two cans of coke on the table Pepsey's sitting at.

There's one of those long Continental-film silences.

'He's . . . er . . . gone somewhere with Jamie and Gary. Boys' night out.'

'So where are the girls?'

'Not sure,' says Pepsey.

'So who are you with?'

'My . . . cousin,' says Pepsey lamely.

She looks at me. She seems very nervous. She seems to be looking over my shoulder at somebody. She gives the merest hint of a nod. Julie catches the gesture and glances round.

'Anyway,' says Pepsey, definitely uncomfortable. 'I'm just off.'

With that she heads for the exit.

'Whoever she's with,' says Julie, 'it isn't her cousin.'

We hold hands all the way back on the bus. Julie gets off soon. Four stops before me.

'I wish tonight could go on forever,' I say.

'A bit of a romantic on the quiet, aren't you?' says Julie.

I shrug, embarrassed. I'm still dying to say the three little words, but I'd come over really pathetic if she doesn't want to hear them.

'Was *he* romantic?'

'Fitz? Give over!'

I'm glad he wasn't. I don't have anything to live up to.

'Have you had any other boyfriends?' I ask.

'No,' says Julie, 'Fitz is it. Unless you count Mark Huxley in the Infants. We starred in the Christmas play together. He was Joseph and I was Mary.'

'Just the one boyfriend? You? Never!'

'I'm telling you the God's honest truth.'

I can't help it, I just lean over and kiss her.

'What was that for?'

'For being you.'

She laughs.

'You're funny, you know that?'

'Funny ha-ha or funny peculiar?'

'Both.'

'Why am I peculiar?'

'Well, you don't try it on.'

'Did Fitz?'

'Not half, I was forever fending him off.'

That I like to hear. I'm careful not to ask if she *always* fended him off. I know Dad is right. Jealousy is definitely unappealing.

'What about you?' she asks. 'How many girlfriends have you had?'

'Just the one. Chloe. Which is none really.'

'What do you mean, none?'

'It was a non-relationship. Rebound stuff. Because of you and Fitz.'

Julie smiles her heart-stopping smile.

'I have to admit I could never see you two together.'

'There's a good reason for that,' I tell her. 'It was a mistake. You know when we got together?'

Julie nods.

'The night of the school disco.'

I smile sadly. The night she got together with Fitz.

'I watched you,' she says.

I shake my head.

'I've been a real idiot,' I say. 'I should have asked you out seven months ago. All that wasted time.'

She moves closer.

'Still, you can start making up for it now, can't you?'

I see those wonderful brown eyes drawing me in. I love you, Julie Carter.

Saturday 3rd March
10.45 p.m.

I'm about to turn into our street. I feel tipsy, intoxicated by the smell of Julie's hair, her perfume, her skin. This is too good to be true. The most beautiful girl in the world with her olive skin and her mane of black hair, and she wants to be with me. In all the movies it's just at this moment, when you think you've finally made it, when life couldn't taste any sweeter, that the mad axeman arrives to cause mayhem. So where's the mad axeman going to come from? I look for grey clouds on the horizon. There's only one; Julie going away to Edinburgh at Easter, and Fitz being there with her.

'I know there's nothing to be worried about,' I say out loud. 'I know it.'

But knowing something isn't the same as believing it, and deep down inside something is gnawing at me.

'Stupid,' I announce to the empty street.

I'm putting my key in the lock when something makes me pause. There's another thought chewing away at the back of my mind, making me uneasy. It doesn't have anything to do with Julie and me, at least I don't think so, but it's these odd occurrences. Emma's little fling for one, and the owner of the other Coke that Pepsey was guarding. They're bothering me for some reason. I'm sure they add up to something. But what?

3

'That you, Terry?'

  'No, Keanu Reeves.'

  'I wish.'

I take my jacket off and hurry into the living-room. The legs of my jeans are soaked right through.

  'Oh Terry, is that all you had on, a thin jacket? Where's that coat I got you?'

  It's at the back of my wardrobe. I wouldn't be seen dead in it. Only hard-core nerds wear a Nanook of the North coat. I'd rather get soaked than be seen in that thing. She'll have me driving huskies next.

  'Well, what have you done with it?'

  'Dunno.'

She snorts but steers away from a row.

  'How was revision?'

I've been revising round at Julie's. I met her after gymnastics and we went to hers. She told me something interesting about Pepsey. That night we saw her at the bowling alley, there was no boys' night out, she'd told Paul she wasn't well. She begged Julie not to give her away, but wouldn't say why. Anyway, about tonight. Julie's been trying to get me to understand vectors. Now I know that there are four notations I've got to learn. I can't actually remember what they are, but I know there are four. I'd make a good Moses. There are ten commandments, I'd tell my people, I don't know what they are but there are definitely ten! So whatever it is you want to do, DON'T!

  'Good,' I say. 'Julie's been explaining vectors.'

104

'Go on then,' says Mum. 'Explain them to me.'

Uh-oh, I didn't see this coming. I have to admit I spent most of the time looking at Julie, the way she crossed her legs, the way a lock of her hair snaked down her throat, the way she ran the tip of her tongue along her upper lip when she was concentrating. OK, so it isn't homework, but it kept me happy.

'They're shown as lines with arrows,' I say with as much authority as I can muster. 'And there are four notations.'

I should have letters after my name. Terry Payne, MK. That's Master of Kiddology. Mum smiles. Easily pleased, my mum. Good job she doesn't have a clue about maths herself, or I'd be well rumbled.

'I'm glad to see you're making an effort,' she says.

Oh, I'm making an effort, all right, an effort not to kill Huey, Duey and Louie.

All the time Julie and I were sitting at the kitchen table they were blowing kisses and making sarcastic remarks. Julie was wearing a sleeveless blouse. I was running a finger down her arm when the three of them came in and started sticking their fingers down their throats and making puking noises. The only kiss Julie gave me all evening was when we stood in the porch on my way out. Still, it's one kiss more than I would have got a few weeks ago. It kept me going all the way home.

'You'd better change out of those clothes,' says Mum.

I nod. On my way upstairs I remember I haven't got any money for my school dinner.

'Have you got my two pounds fifty?' I ask.

'There's some change in my fleece,' says Mum. 'It's hanging up.'

I feel in her pockets and pull out three pound coins. Stuck between them is a scrap of paper.

It reads: 'Richard – 426 0010.'

Richard? I don't know any Richard. Then the penny drops. She went for a drink again last night, straight after jogging.

'Did you get it?' Mum calls.

'Yes.'

In fact, I got more than I bargained for. I slip the note back in her pocket.

Wednesday 7th March
7.35 p.m.

Bummer!

Just when I was listening to Des Lynam explaining the importance of Panathanaikos v United in the Champions' League, Dad prised it out of me, the identity of Mum's new boyfriend.

'Richard?' he says. 'I don't know any Richard.'

'I think he's in her jogging club.'

Dad must be picturing this really fit hunk, a cross between Jude Law and Linford Christie, because he starts sucking in his belly.

'At least it isn't one of my mates,' he says. 'I couldn't cope with that.'

'It's not like she's having an affair,' I say. 'You are divorced, remember. Mum's a free woman.'

I'm only repeating what Julie said to me in school. Somehow, I don't think I'm helping. For the next ten minutes Dad's really quiet. It's a relief when the match kicks off.

But not much of a relief.

I've been looking forward to this game. Tonight's the night we're supposed to show our class and sweep away the opposition. Tonight's the night we're supposed to book our place in the quarter-finals. Only it doesn't go to plan.

Twenty-four minutes into a game we seem to be treating as a friendly, Panathanaikos take the lead with a screamer of a shot from outside the area.

'What are they playing at?' groans Dad.

One thing's for certain. It isn't football. We can hardly string two passes together. We're listless and, frankly, the Greeks are playing us off the park. Time and again they slice open our defence. It's embarrassing. Football is supposed to give you a chance to be part of something bigger than you, a thing of pride. All I can think of when the half-time whistle goes is how I can hold my head up in school tomorrow. The Manc-baiters will be out in force, that's for sure.

The second half isn't much better. Even though we put a bit more pressure on, we still can't open them up and they keep launching sweeping counter-attacks that threaten to kill us off.

'I don't believe this,' says Dad, head in hands.

Just like he can't believe Mum is going out with a marathon-running hunk called Richard.

'That's the end of normal time,' I say, glancing at my watch. We're into stoppage time. Four minutes added.

'Come on, lads,' I say. 'Remember Barcelona.'

Sheringham and Solskjaer. European champions. Doing the conga down the Ramblas.

'There's still time.'

'No miracles tonight,' says Dad.

Fortunately he's wrong. After ninety-two minutes Paul Scholes hits a sweet shot into the back of the net. He's spared United's blushes with an undeserved 1–1 draw. The upshot of a disappointing night: so long as we don't lose by more than 2–0 at home to Sturm Graz next Tuesday, we're through.

On my way home I phone Julie. Just to hear her voice. I can't believe how wonderful she is, she doesn't even ask why I phoned, but she makes me glad I did. She puts a smile back on my face.

Saturday 10th March
10.00 a.m.

The car park is packed. There are coaches from all over the country. I'm here at Everton Park sports centre to support Julie . . . and to keep an eye on Fitz. OK, I know what I said about jealousy being a complete turn-off but Fitz would do anything to split me and Julie up. So I'm not giving him a chance. He'll use the fact that his kid sister Hayley is taking part to come down and make a nuisance of himself, but don't worry, I have a counter-nuisance strategy prepared. It's called Don't Let Julie Out Of My Sight.

'Terry, you made it!'

It's Julie. She throws her arms round my neck and kisses me. Kelly rolls her eyes and makes gagging noises. Pepsey just looks on. She's been subdued ever since we saw her at the bowling alley. I'd love to know what her big secret is.

'What's he doing here?' asks Kelly. 'This isn't a boyfriend event. My Gary isn't coming.'

'He isn't interested,' says Julie. 'Terry is.'

Yes, interested in you.

In the foyer, Julie gets me a pass. I'm about to follow her through to the hall where the display is taking place, when my mobile goes.

'I'd better answer,' I say. 'See you inside.'

I step back through the doors.

'Yes?'

'It's me.'

'Hi Bobby, what's up?'

'I'm outside the stupid registry office.'

Of course, it's his mum's wedding day. She's getting hitched to Slughead, the big guy with the cocker spaniel that pukes over Bobby's bed.

'You still don't like him then?'

What comes out of the phone isn't a reply but this really long BLEURRCH! sound.

'He's a complete creepazoid, Terry. This is the worst day of my life.'

'I thought that was when you found out Emma had been seeing someone else?'

'Thanks for cheering me up, Terry.'

'Sorry.'

'It's not your fault.'

'Is Emma with you?' I ask.

'No, but she's coming to the reception. You sure you can't come?'

They're having a big do in the evening.

'Sorry Bob,' I say. 'It clashes with this gymnastics disco.'

'But they're holding it at Anfield! You can't go in there. It's like a turkey signing up to get stuffed.'

'I've got to, Bobby. You understand.'

He gives a long sigh.

'Yes, I understand. The lovely Julie.'

'Yes,' I say. 'The lovely Julie.'

Saturday 10th March
11.30 a.m.

It's Julie's turn to perform. I watch her and the nineteen other members of the club walk out in their shimmering silver leotards. Looking at Julie, I can't believe she's actually going out with me. I keep on saying that, don't I? I mean, this girl is incredible. All the way through the first part of the dance routine I've got my eyes glued to her, sleek, lovely Julie. Just once, her eyes meet mine and she smiles. It's a breathtaking smile, kind of proud and kind of embarrassed and one hundred per cent beautiful. I glance round at where Fitz is sitting, two rows behind me and to my left. He scowls. Mrs Carter, who is sitting next to me, notices and chuckles.

'You're making him very jealous,' she whispers.

'I know,' I say.

Then, jokingly but also deadly serious: 'Good, isn't it?'

Mrs Carter winks. She's the only member of the family who isn't a card-carrying member of the Fitz fan club. On the quiet I think she had him down as the lousy groper he is.

The second part of the routine has begun: *Heaven must be missing an angel*. It's got an *Aw* factor of nine, mainly down to the younger girls, and a palpitation factor of ten, totally down to Julie. When they're finished I clap until my hands sting. Fitz is still scowling.

I meet Julie outside. There's a little catering stall and we have bacon sandwiches, doughnuts and fizzy drinks.

'Aren't you gymnasts supposed to eat healthily?' I ask. 'Pasta and chicken, that sort of thing?'

Julie laughs, dabbing bacon fat off her chin with a paper napkin.

'Supposed to is right,' she says. 'I even tried to be a vegetarian last year, you know, but I couldn't resist the smell of bacon.'

'You were fantastic in there,' I say enthusiastically.

'Thanks,' says Julie, 'but it wasn't that good. We missed one of our balances.'

'Did you? I didn't notice.'

'That,' says Julie, teasing me in that gentle way of hers, 'is because you were staring at my legs.'

'I was not!'

'Were too! And that's not all you were staring at.'

I'm wondering what to say, when she gives me a hug.

'Don't worry,' she says, 'I'm flattered.'

Her voice drops to a whisper: 'I fancy you rotten too.'

She fancies me! Fancies me *rotten*! This girl is too good to be true. I see Fitz come out on to the steps in front of the sports centre. He sees us sitting on the wall and shakes his head before going back inside. Six Guns says Fitz will be at training this week. The showdown is coming.

Saturday 10th March
8.30 p.m.

Now I know what Luke Skywalker felt like when he penetrated the Death Star. I've just entered Anfield, heart of the Evil Empire. Mum's dropped me off so I've got to tread enemy territory all on my own. There are all these bouncers ushering people past the Bill Shankly this and the Bob Paisley that. I'm at the heart of the Beast. I'm looking around for Julie, but I can't see her. I'm hovering uncertainly outside the function room where they're holding the disco when Kelly and Pepsey walk through the doors. They're both dressed up to the nines and look much older than sixteen.

'You look nice,' I say.

I've got to butter them up. They're Julie's best mates.

Kelly gives me a withering glance which says: *Whose shoe did you come in on?* Pepsey keeps shtum.

'Have you seen Julie?' I ask.

'She isn't here yet,' says Kelly, before walking away without so much as a by-your-leave.

She's just about to disappear into the function room when she turns round and says to one of the bouncers, a particularly gorilla-like individual with a shaved head: 'See him? He supports Man U.'

Kelly may look like Sabrina, the teenage witch, but she's got a voice like flipping Pavarotti. Every head in the place turns to look at me.

To my relief, Julie walks in at that very moment. She's wearing black trousers which look like they've been painted on and a sparkly crop top (I think that's what they're called) that shows her bare midriff. My throat goes dry. We're talking Gobi Desert.

'Julie,' I croak, before clearing my throat. 'I mean, Julie you look . . .'

110

'What?'

How do I answer this without drooling?

'Gorgeous.'

'That'll do nicely,' she says, doing a mock curtsey. 'Where are the others?'

'Dunno,' I say. 'I just got here.'

I don't tell her about Kelly. There's no point bad-mouthing her best friend.

'There they are!'

All of a sudden there are all these teenage girls flocking together, hugging and talking all at once. Suddenly I feel very left out.

'Terry,' says Julie. 'I'm going to have a couple of dances with the girls. You don't mind watching our stuff, do you?'

I shake my head and sit next to a chair piled high with coats and handbags. I've played gooseberry in my time, but never to a dozen females! Fitz enters with Hayley. Hayley repeats the flocking, hugging, talking at once routine with the younger girls and similarly disappears in the direction of the dance floor, leaving me and Fitz alone in a corner of the bar. We look at each other briefly, wondering what to do next. Eventually, Gary Tudor walks in and he and Fitz go to the bar. I crane my neck to see the girls but they're out of sight round the corner. Julie's couple of dances last twenty-five minutes, and even when they do return it's only to take liquid refreshment and disappear back to the dance floor.

'Sorry to leave you hanging on here,' says Julie. 'But I won't be long. You do understand, don't you?'

'Sure,' I say. 'You enjoy yourself.'

And I sit there with this big stone in my heart, wishing I'd never come at all. I look around and I can't see Fitz. What if . . . no, don't even think it, Terry lad. Another twenty minutes have gone when he appears.

'Left you on your own, has she? Bad sign that, mate.'

Then he's gone again.

I can't remember when I felt more alone.

Saturday 10th March
9.15 p.m.

I can't see Julie or Fitz. My mind is working overtime. How could she do this to me? Another five minutes and I'm walking out of here.

Saturday 10th March
9.25 p.m.

OK, five *more* minutes.

Saturday 10th March
9.33 p.m.

Right, that does it. She's with him. I *know* she is.

Fancy me rotten, does she?

Well, it looks like it, doesn't it? I've made a complete idiot of myself this time.

Saturday, 10th March
9.34 p.m.

It's her!

'Oh Terry, I'm so sorry. I didn't notice the time. Come on, you've got my complete and undivided attention for the rest of the night. Hey Fitz.'

He gets up from a table. It seems that's where he's been all the time. I breathe a sigh of relief. I've been torturing myself for nothing.

'Watch the coats, will you? I'm going to have a dance with my feller.'

I watch Fitz's face. It's worth all the waiting. He looks crushed.

Sunday 11th March
1 p.m.

Bobby's been round to my house for some TLC. Mum's fed him and I've counselled him. I should be a priest. I do good confession.

'That bad, eh?' I say, doing my best to sound sympathetic, which is hard when you're hearing the story for the third time.

'Would you believe it?' Bobby says. 'She puked over my shoe.'

She is Lady, Slughead's cocker spaniel. Not Emma, you understand.

'Maybe she's got a delicate stomach,' I suggest.

'So why's it only delicate around me?' Bobby demands. 'And what moron brings his dog to a wedding reception?'

'The moron your mum's just married.'

'That's when it all started to go wrong,' says Bobby, burying his face in his hands. 'Emma stuck up for the dog, I mentioned the mystery boyfriend and she walked out on me.'

'Have you phoned her?' I ask.

'Three times,' says Bobby. 'She just hangs up.'

I check my watch. I've got to make a move soon if I'm going to watch the Tranmere–Liverpool game on TV with Julie.

'Look Bobby . . .'

'It's over, isn't it Terry?'

'Maybe, but Bobby . . .'

'I can't let it end like this, though.'

'No, Bobby.'

'You think she's worth it, don't you, Terry?'

'Yes Bobby.'

'I know I'm a prat.'

'Yes Bobby.'

He frowns.

'I mean, no Bobby.'

'Have you been listening to me?'

'Of course I have.'

For two hours actually!

'So what do I do, Terry?'

I pull a face.

'I don't know, Bobby, but if you want my advice the last thing you do is bring up this other lad. That's just suicidal.'

'You're right,' says Bobby, brightening.

He stands up and I reach for my coat. Just as quickly he sits down again. Reluctantly, I put my jacket down.

'But what if she won't see me? What do you think, Terry?'

You want to know what I think, Bobby? I think you're one

pain-in-the-neck loser right now. I don't say that, though. He's the pain-in-the-neck loser who listened to me all those months I was pining after Julie. I do my duty and say:

'Why not run through it again for me, Bobby?'

Sunday 11th March
2.46 p.m.

Julie lets me in.

'Sorry I'm late,' I say. 'I had to nursemaid Bobby.'

'Is this about Emma?'

I nod.

'You're just in time for the second half,' she says, leading the way into the living room. On my way down on the bus I had this picture in my head of Julie and me alone in the living-room. I'm sorely disappointed. The whole family is glued to the screen. I have to sit on the carpet with my back against the leather couch.

'What's the score?'

'Two–nil to Liverpool.'

I grimace. I just can't help it.

'You'd better keep him quiet,' says Gerard, noticing.

He talks about me as if I'm a naughty puppy, or a particularly foul-mouthed parrot.

The match has hardly resumed when Yates meets a terrific cross and heads home for Tranmere.

'Yiss!' I shout, raising my fist.

Gerard, Josh and John-Joe raise their fists, and not in celebration.

Five minutes later Steve Gerrard puts Liverpool 3–1 up. The living-room erupts and I get mobbed. Everybody's rubbing my head and hitting me with cushions and asking me the score.

'All over bar the shouting,' says Mr Carter, making no effort not to gloat.

It isn't. After fifty-seven minutes the Tranmere substitute Allison scores with his first touch.

'Yiss!' I shout.

Tranmere two, Liverpool three.

Gerard, Josh and John-Joe glare at me.

'Can't you shut him up?' they ask.

Brain to mouth: if you know what's good for you, you'll keep quiet.

After seventy-six minutes Tranmere are denied an obvious penalty. There's no way I'm keeping quiet.

'See that?' I say. 'Hyppia was all over Allison. Blatant penalty.'

Gerard, Josh and John-Joe snarl menacingly.

Brain to mouth: shut up, shut up, shut up.

Two minutes later Tranmere are denied a second penalty for hand ball.

'Oh, I don't believe this,' I protest. 'What's that ref's name, Gerard flipping Houllier?'

Brain to mouth: That's it, I'm off home. You're on your own.

Then, in the eightieth minute, McAllister goes down and is awarded a penalty. Robbie Fowler scores. Four–two to Liverpool and game over. Ten minutes later the ref blows the final whistle.

'Go on,' says Gerard, 'say something. Anything. Make our day.'

Say nothing, absolutely nothing.

'You only won because of the ref,' I say.

Next moment I'm buried under three Scousers all belting me with cushions.

'Had enough?' asks John-Joe.

'Tranmere should have . . .'

More battering.

'. . . had a . . .'

Bludgeoning into submission.

'. . . penalty.'

They finally let me up. Julie and her mum and dad are laughing themselves silly. I can't help but join in.

Sunday 11th March
9.00 p.m.

Julie and me at the bus stop. Drizzle. Kisses. The smell of coconut on her hair.

'You smell nice,' I say.

'It's my conditioner,' she says. 'Have you recovered from your ragging?'

'Just about,' I say.

'I think they're starting to like you,' says Julie.

'*That's* liking me!'

Julie nods.

'And I like you too, a lot.'

This is it. The time to say the three little words. I'm still trying to pluck up the courage when my bus comes. We kiss and I climb on board. I wave to Julie through drizzle-flecked windows and kick myself all the way home.

4

I walk to school through driving rain. I still won't wear my Nanook of the North coat so I'm making do with my fleece and an Adidas baseball cap. They don't give me much protection against the downpour, but at least I don't look like a nerd. Something else insulates me against the storm. United dispatched Sturm Graz 3–0 last night. We're through to the quarter-finals of the Champions' League. I look down the hill towards Liverpool. It isn't much more than a puddle of grey under the rain, but suddenly the sun comes out from behind the clouds, a brilliant gleaming sphere riding the banks of purple. It turns the half-deserted streets into a giant mirror. The few pedestrians who are struggling up the hill are no more than silhouettes against the blinding sunlight. When a bus stops more silhouettes start to make their way across the road.

'Terry!'

One of them is Julie. I shield my eyes and smile to see her running towards me. She draws me under her umbrella and we kiss, faces illuminated by the eerie light. She warms me against the chill of the morning. Kelly is standing a couple of steps away. All I see is her shoes, but I know it's her. The shoes seem to snarl at me. Besides, I can hear the resentment working through her, like the hiss of air brakes. She's never far away from Julie, guardian of the Scouse flame. The three of us walk towards the school gates, Julie and me arm in arm, Kelly kind of semi-detached and hissing.

'Do you fancy coming round tonight?' I ask. 'I'm baby-sitting our Amy. Mum's going out again with the jogging club.'

'I thought that was Mondays and Fridays.'

'It is. Seems they've got a club meeting.'

Julie pulls a face.

'Meeting? About jogging? Sounds fishy to me.'

Funny, I've had the stench of haddock in my nostrils too. I'm guessing the attendance of this meeting will be a grand total of two: Mum and Richard.

'So do you fancy it?' I ask. 'We can watch Arsenal against Bayern Munich. You know, support the Germans.'

'How romantic!' sneers Kelly.

Julie winks at me. I love that. She's pulled me into a conspiracy of two.

'It's a date,' she says, 'so long as Mum and Dad don't mind. We can do some simultaneous equations before kick-off.'

At the thought of the approaching exams I feel the angel of death passing over me.

'Do we have to?'

'Terry Payne, I'll get you through GCSE Maths if it's the last thing I do.'

I see a tombstone. Julie Carter RIP. She died, broken on the rock of another's stupidity.

'Deal?'

'OK, it's a deal.'

Just then Kelly spots Gary and detaches herself. I watch her go then turn to Julie.

'She still doesn't like me, does she?'

'She'll come round,' says Julie.

'Sure about that?' I ask.

'Yes, sure as I'm sitting here on this unicycle.'

Wednesday 14th March
7.45 p.m.

'What an awful match,' I say.

'They're all awful,' says Amy.

She looks at Julie as if to say: *how can a girl like football?*

Arsenal have scraped through, so that's three English teams, three Spanish teams, one German and one Turkish team in the quarter-finals of the Champions' League.

'We'll be joining you next year,' says Julie. 'Houllier's got us sorted.'

'Maybe.'

It's something I've always dreaded, Liverpool catching up with Man U. Dad's told me what it was like in the eighties, living in their shadow. We don't want to go back to that. But, with every week that passes, they seem to be catching us up.

'Fancy coming round again for the Liverpool–Porto game?' I say.

'Can't,' says Julie. 'It's the gymnastics club tomorrow night. It's less than a month before we go to Scotland.'

'Oh yes, I forgot.'

I feel the stab of a single icicle in my heart. Edinburgh, where Julie will be for three days. Fitz too.

'What do you do in the evenings?' I ask.

I hope she doesn't notice the green-eyed monster rearing its ugly head.

'The first night we just crash out. It's a heck of a coach ride.'

'And the second?'

'It's like the Ministrada. There's a disco for all the gymnasts.'

That's what I was afraid of. I remember Julie and Fitz dancing a slowie that terrible night last year when they got together. The icicle becomes a shard of glass slicing through my peace of mind.

'And you don't need to worry,' says Julie, 'I won't be dancing with any of those big Scottish hunks.'

Scottish hunks! Who said anything about Scottish hunks?

It was bad enough worrying about Fitz, now Julie's being courted by a mob of Bravehearts. I see all these hairy guys with blue faces. Gross!

'Anyway,' says Julie. 'I've got to go. I promised Mum I'd be home before half past eight.'

'I'll walk you to . . .'

I remember Amy.

'It's all right,' says Julie. 'You stay with Amy.'

I look at Amy, willing her to go to her room. She fails to take the hint.

'Amy,' I say, 'haven't you got anything to do?'

She stands, looking at me.

'No.'

'Homework or something?'

119

'No.'

'Anything?'

The penny drops.

'Oh,' she says, 'you want smoochies.'

Julie giggles at my obvious discomfort.

'I'll make myself scarce then,' says Amy, grinning mischievously at Julie.

'I hate girls,' I seethe as she runs upstairs giggling.

'Even this girl?' asks Julie, nibbling at my bottom lip.

'No,' I say, 'just little girls.'

'I was a little girl once,' says Julie.

I smile and run my hands over her ribcage and hips.

'That was a long time ago.'

Friday 16th March
12.10 p.m.

'Have you heard the draw?'

I press my mobile to my ear and smile. It's Dad. No: *Hi Terry.* No: *How's your day been?* He just cuts to the chase. The draw for the Champions' League quarter finals.

'Not Real Madrid?'

'No, but not much better. It's Bayern Munich.'

A rerun of the final two years ago. Bayern will be up for that one. Hungry for revenge.

'Grudge match,' I say.

'Definitely. Oh yes, and Liverpool have drawn Barcelona in the UEFA Cup.'

I pass the news on to Julie who's standing next to me just outside the school gates. She purses her lips.

'Tough one.'

'That your girlfriend?' asks Dad.

'Yes, say hello Julie.'

Julie shouts a breezy greeting.

'I never believed a son of mine would end up going out with a Scouser,' says Dad.

I smile at Julie.

'Dad, I know what you mean.'

'How's your mum?'

'Fine.'

120

There's a silence at the other end. I know what Dad wants to say: *Any more on this Richard?*

'I'll see you tomorrow,' I say. 'We can listen to the United–Leicester game.'

'Yes, see you then.'

My face must betray my emotions because Julie asks:

'Is he going on about your Mum and her boyfriend again?'

I nod.

'I think it's getting serious. I've been trying not to believe it, but you can tell, can't you?'

'Can you?'

'She comes in all flushed. She looks . . . younger.'

'Sounds like love all right,' says Julie.

'So how do I tell Dad?'

Julie doesn't get to answer because Bobby and Emma arrive. I see Emma's face fall. For some reason she doesn't like Julie one bit.

'Fancy going into town for half an hour?' asks Bobby.

I glance at Julie. She shakes her head.

'I've got a couple of things to do in the library,' she says.

I look at Bobby and shrug my shoulders.

'Fair enough,' he says. 'See you later.'

The moment they're out of earshot I turn to Julie.

'What was that about?' I ask. 'You haven't got anything to do in the library.'

'No, it's Emma. She's got a real downer on me.'

'Any idea why?'

Julie shakes her head.

'I don't know what I've done wrong, but she doesn't want to know me at all.'

I look down the road. Bobby and Emma are just turning the corner. What is going on?

Saturday 17th March
5.30 p.m.

I'm in worry mode.

For starters, Barthez has done his hamstring. It was the one blemish on an otherwise satisfying afternoon at Old Trafford. The Reds dispatched Leicester 2–0 to go 17 points clear at the top of the Premiership. But now Barthez could be missing against both Liverpool and Bayern Munich.

Which brings me on to Worry Number Two. We visit Anfield the Saturday after next. I just couldn't stand it if they did the double on us.

And so to Worry Number Three. Dad is really down about Mum and this Richard bloke. That's right, he managed to prize it out of me at half-time.

'What's he like?' he asked.

'Dunno.'

'What does he do for a living?'

'Dunno.'

'How serious is Sharon about him?'

'Dunno.'

Actually, I've got a pretty good idea. Mum didn't get in until half past eleven last night. Her face was flushed. She was glowing like a lamp with a red shade. She's spending more and more time with him. I may be making a mint from the baby-sitting money, but I can't say I like it.

Then there's Worry Number Four. Bobby came round this morning. He's really cut up about Emma. He thinks she's still seeing this other lad. I can't believe this is the same Bobby. He didn't even give me the statistics for cheating by sixteen-year-old girls. Suddenly he's had a good mood-ectomy. He's really got it bad for Emma.

The more convinced he gets that she's messing him around, the more he wants to be with her. Confused? Me too.

Finally, there's Worry Number Five. The big one. That, of course, is Julie. You're probably wondering what I've got to worry about. But does she still feel something for Fitz? I mean, they did go out for seven months. That's got to mean something. How can you be sure what's going on in somebody else's mind? How do you know they feel the same about you as you do about them? I can't get it out of my mind. Three weeks tonight, Julie will be up in Edinburgh, and you can be sure Fitz won't be far away. And it isn't just Fitz. What about all those blue-faced Bravehearts queuing up for a dance? I remember that gymnastics club from Glasgow Julie was raving about at the Ministrada. They'll be there, all hunky and hormonal.

'A penny for them,' says Dad.

'I beg your pardon?'

'I was wondering what you were thinking. You were miles away.'

'Oh nothing.'

'Doing anything tonight?'

'I'm going to the cinema with Julie.'

'I hear she's a good looking girl,' says Dad, with a wink. 'You'd better keep your eye on her.'

My head snaps round.

'What do you mean?'

I said that a bit too quickly, and a bit too loud.

'Whoa,' says Dad. 'Only joking, son.'

I look away quickly.

'Is everything all right?'

I think so. I *hope* so.

5

I forgot Worry Number Six, Fitz getting match fit again. Well,
he's over the broken ankle and I reckon he'll be gunning for
me tonight in training. I loosen my tie and unbutton my school
shirt. I notice Fitz watching me. He's got this slight curl of a
smile on his thin lips like he's got something in store for me.
Gary's got his eye on me too and he is also smiling. I've got
used to getting changed on my own and being left out of the
dressing room banter. It's been my punishment for injuring
Fitz at Christmas. But until tonight there has been a bit of a
thaw. Some of the lads have actually been talking to me. Not
tonight. I'm back on the outside looking in. The boy who
crocked John Fitzpatrick. Mr Unpopular. Paul Scully goes over
to Fitz.

'Make sure you've got your shinpads on properly,' he says.

It's meant to be overheard. I finish getting changed. The
only thing that is going to get me through the next hour is the
thought of Julie back home baby-sitting Amy. She'll be there
waiting for me when I get in. There's nothing Fitz can do that
can take the shine off that, the promise of Julie's brown eyes.

'Come on lads,' shouts Six Guns. 'Look lively.'

Nobody's in any hurry to get out on the field. Sleet has been
flickering through the air all day and now that it's late
afternoon it's turning to snow.

'Look lively!' snorts Jamie Sneddon. 'He should have called
it off.'

'I heard that,' shouts Six Guns from outside. 'You lads are
too rotten molly-coddled. Get out there and warm up.'

We go through the motions. Jogging, various exercises, tuck

jumps. But what everybody's looking forward to is the five-a-side. Everybody except me. The sympathy is all for Fitz, back from injury. I'll be lucky if I get a single pass.

Wednesday 21st March
5.00 p.m.

I got more than a pass. Fitz ran his studs down the back of my calf, really sneaky, then five minutes later he caught me on the ankle. I think Jamie saw him but he probably thinks I had it coming. I sit rubbing my calf, then ease my sock over my gashed ankle. Finally, I get dressed. Fitz is outside. The others are half-way across the field.

'What do you want?' I ask.

'I'm letting you know,' says Fitz. 'That's just for starters. I'm going to get my own back for what you did.'

'What I did! You know it was an accident. You were trying to do me.'

Fitz sneers.

'What if I was? It's my word against yours. I still ended up missing weeks of the season. I'm going to get you. You can count on it.'

He is setting off towards the school when anger flares inside me.

'I know what's eating you,' I call after him. 'Julie's with me, and you're jealous.'

Fitz spins round. I know I've struck a chord.

'Think what you want, slimeball,' he says. 'But believe me, that isn't over either.'

He hoists his bag over his shoulder.

'Not by a long chalk.'

Wednesday 21st March
5.15 p.m.

I'm at the Fusilier before I notice how far I've walked. I haven't been aware of my surroundings at all, only Fitz's words:

That isn't over either.

Suddenly all I can think about is Edinburgh.

I bet he's bluffing. He's got to be. It's all talk. Julie wouldn't do that to me. But they've got history. I remember something Mum said once: *You never get over your first love*. And that was Fitz. Julie's first love was John stinking, dog's breath, dirtbag, weasel eyes Fitzpatrick.

And whose fault is that? Mine. All the time she was waiting for me to ask her out I just stood there like a wet Wednesday with my foot in my mouth. If she does go back to him I've only got myself to blame.

But she can't go back to him! She can't. She mustn't. For a few moments I imagine myself begging her not to go to Edinburgh. But what good would that do? It would just make me look like even more of a loser than I already am. Jealousy – the biggest turn-off. No, I can't do it. I'd be telling her I don't trust her. She'd be hurt. And I do trust her. I love the bones of the girl. And yet . . . that little voice won't go away.

It isn't over.

Wednesday 21st March
5.25 p.m.

'Are you all right?' asks Julie.

I'm not putting my full weight on my right ankle. That tackle by Fitz didn't just break the skin. I think it's swelling.

'Yes, just a little something from Fitz.'

'Oh, you two haven't been at it again, have you?'

'Us two! What do you mean, us two? I didn't do anything.'

Julie tries to laugh it off.

'It's not funny,' I say. 'Julie, trust me over this. I didn't break Fitz's ankle on purpose. He went for me. Now he's doing it again. Well, do you believe me or not?'

'Terry, it isn't a big deal.'

I shake my head furiously.

'It is to me. Fitz started it. You've got to believe me.'

I can see by the look on Julie's face that she wants me to drop it. But I can't. I hate myself for doing it, but I carry it on, insisting that she believes me. Then I really drop a brick.

'Don't tell me you're taking sides with Fitz,' I say.

'Don't be stupid,' says Julie.

She's getting impatient. But do I take the hint? Of course

not. I just keep on at her, like a dog with a bone, until I really shoot myself in the foot.

'You've still got a soft spot for him, haven't you?'

Julie stares at me. Her eyes have gone hard.

'Is that what this is all about? You think there's still something between me and Fitz?'

Don't answer, says my better self.

'You went out with him for long enough.'

D'oh!

'I've told you what happened,' says Julie. 'I never really fell for him.'

Let it drop, says my better self.

'Yes? Is that why it took you six months to dump him?'

D'oh!

'Terry, if you're going to be like this I'm off home.'

Now let it drop, you dufus. But I don't. No, I open my fat mouth and say the stupidest thing I can imagine.

'I bet he can't wait for Edinburgh.'

D'oh, d'oh and double d'oh! The moment the words are out of my mouth, I want to stuff them back in. Julie's looking at me, really hurt. Tears start to well up in her brown eyes and she turns suddenly, grabs her coat and runs for the door.

'Julie,' I cry. 'Don't go. I didn't mean it.'

'So why say it?' she sobs.

With that, she's gone.

Wednesday 21st March
5.35 p.m.

I'm still standing in the hallway, my body slack with shock, my arms limp by my sides, when Mum comes in.

'Was that Julie I saw running down the street?' she asks.

I nod. I feel numb all over. It's our first row.

'Is something wrong?'

I explain what's just happened.

'Oh Terry, you silly lad. Go after her. She might still be at the bus stop.'

I don't need telling twice. I fly out of the house and into the blowy darkness. I'm only wearing a T-shirt, jogging pants and trainers. The wind cuts through me but I don't care. I've got to get to Julie before the bus does. I'm sprinting for all I'm worth, the sleet stinging my face. Why couldn't I pay attention to my inner voice? There he was, the real me, telling me to behave myself. But would I listen? No. Instead, I have to take notice of the green-eyed monster. What if I've ruined everything? I'm running round the bend in the road within striking distance of the stop when the bus overtakes me.

Please let there be a lot of other passengers. Anything to hold the bus up.

But Julie's the only one at the stop.

'Julie!' I cry.

She doesn't hear me. Or maybe she does. Either way she gets on the bus without turning round.

'Wait.'

The doors start to close. Oh no you don't! I fling myself at the doors and sprawl full length on the floor.

'What the . . . ?'

The driver looks shocked. I shove my hand in my pocket and drop some loose change in his hand. Without waiting for the ticket I walk towards Julie. I'm aware that my clothes are steaming.

'But where are you going?' asks the driver.

'I don't know yet,' I say as I stand panting by Julie's seat.

Look at me. Please look at me.

'I'll issue you with a 35p ticket,' says the driver.

Oh, shut up about your stupid ticket. My life's on the line here.

'Sure, whatever.'

I slide into the seat next to Julie. She's looking straight ahead.

'I'm really sorry.'

Still looking ahead.

'I'm an idiot.'

'You got that right.'

Oh joy! She's talking to me.

'Hit me,' I say, offering my chin. 'Go on, hit me.'

Julie turns towards me.

'You don't really think I'd . . . ? Not with Fitz.'

'Of course not. I trust you. You know I do.'

That's not good enough, says the sensible voice. Talk to her. Tell her how you feel.

128

So that's what I try to do. Haltingly. Stumblingly.

'It's just . . . You get feelings. You don't want to, but they just come.'

We talk all the way to her stop. I answer all her questions. I talk till I'm red in the face. That's when I remember.

'Mum!'

'Pardon?'

'She thought I was only going down to the stop. She'll wonder where on earth I've got to.'

Wednesday 21st March
6.15 p.m.

'You're where?'

Mum's cry of disbelief almost takes the top of my head off.

'Julie's.'

For the second time in an hour I'm trying to explain myself, this time on the phone to Mum.

'But you haven't even got a coat. Aren't you freezing?'

I admit that I am. Right now, I'd even wear the Nanook of the North coat.

'Do you want me to pick you up?' she asks. 'Amy won't mind.'

I hear Amy's voice in the background: *Says who?*

'Julie's brother says he'll lend me a coat,' I say. 'I'll be back by half past seven.'

'See that you are,' says Mum.

I put the phone down and see Gerard coming towards me with a jacket. It's a couple of sizes too small, but that isn't the most important thing. It's the logo. Liverpool FC.

'I'm not wearing that!' I say.

'Why not?' he asks all innocent.

'Gerard,' says Julie. 'Get him something he can wear.'

Gerard climbs the stairs chuckling all the way. Josh and John-Joe join in.

'They're only winding you up,' says Julie. 'He'll find something.'

I pull her close.

'Am I forgiven?'

'Of course you are.'

129

I go to kiss her. She draws away.

'But, Terry . . .'

'Yes?'

'Don't ever do that again. Either you trust me, or we're finished.'

I nod guiltily.

'I'll be a good boy.'

I put on my best chastened toddler look. Julie giggles.

'Ok. Now, let's have that kiss.'

Out of the corner of my eye, I can see Huey, Duey and Louie pulling faces. I don't care. I've got out of jail.

Just.

6

I never thought it would come to this, me and half a dozen Scousers watching England play. Yes, I'm round at Julie's. Dad wanted me to watch the Finland game round his, but let's face it, in two weeks Julie is off to Edinburgh so I'm determined to be as high-profile as I can. When she's surrounded by Fitz and all those blue-faced Bravehearts, I want her to remember her loving boyfriend back home. So hard luck, Dad. When it comes down to a choice between the High King of Victim Rock and the most beautiful girl in the world, you're always going to take second place. Dad took it OK, no big guilt trip or anything, but there was no disguising the disappointment in his voice. He's all out of luck. Since he ditched Mule and decided he was still in love with Mum, his life has taken a real nosedive. He just can't believe they're divorced. Just about the biggest thing that's ever happened to him and it kind of crept up while he wasn't looking. As for Mum getting into a size twelve and finding herself a hunky running-machine of a boyfriend, he's devastated. Not because she's got a size twelve figure, of course, but because she's showing off to somebody else. Suddenly he's the major loser.

'You OK?' asks Julie, budging up on the couch until her thigh's touching mine.

'I am now,' I tell her, putting poor old Dad to the back of my mind.

Poor old Bobby too. He wanted to watch the match round at Dad's. Anything to escape the rest of his life. Emma's still acting distant and Slughead's cocker spaniel's taken to peeing by the side of his wardrobe. Bobby says it's a vendetta. Of

131

course, it could just be a weak bladder. You know what I told Bobby? *If your room smells like a kennel don't be surprised when the dog makes itself at home there.*

He might be my best mate, but if Dad isn't going to drag me away from Julie, Bobby certainly isn't.

'I don't think Beckham's the man to captain England,' says Gerard pointedly, as Beckham leads the side out at Anfield.

'No charisma,' says Josh, glancing in my direction.

'Doesn't talk enough,' says John-Joe, making a big, goofy face at me. *'Can't* talk enough.'

'Exactly,' says Gerard, 'IQ of a lobotomised sprout.'

I grit my teeth. Maybe I should have gone round to Dad's after all.

'I wonder which Manc's going to ruin our chances this time,' says Gerard.

It's as if Fitz is right here in the room, taunting me. Now, that's an uncomfortable thought, a bad omen for Edinburgh. Josh and John-Joe join in the Manc-baiting. They dredge up all the old stuff, how Beckham got sent off against Argentina and got us knocked out of the World Cup, how Phil Neville gave away that penalty and got us eliminated from Euro 2000. To hear them talk you'd think there was a Manc conspiracy against the national team! They even have a go at me about Gary Neville, Paul Scholes and Andy Cole being the only players who don't sing the national anthem. Like I give a damn! A few minutes into the game, Beckham is on the way to shutting them up.

'Not a captain, eh?' I say. 'So explain today's performance. He's playing brilliantly.'

But the anti-Manc hysteria reaches fever pitch in the twenty-seventh minute when Gary Neville deflects a Finnish header into his own net. 1–0 to Finland.

'Told you,' crows Gerard. 'Now both the Neville brothers have done it. No wonder they don't sing the national anthem. They're too busy playing for the other side!'

He makes up this stupid song called Finland, my Finland. Funny guy!

Fortunately, England end the first half on fire. Beckham and Neville combine to set up Michael Owen's equaliser.

'There,' I say. 'Two United players made the goal.'

'Yes,' says Julie. 'But it took one of ours to score it.'

I grimace. She thinks Michael Owen's cute. Five minutes into the second half the misery of Gary Neville's own goal is well and truly buried. David Beckham turns captain fantastic and drills home a superb right-foot drive. When the final whistle goes and England have won 2–1, I have the audacity to shout:

'Beckham, king of the Kop!'

While the others boo and hiss, I think of next Saturday's Liverpool–United match on the very same Anfield turf where England have just revived their slim chances of World Cup qualification. That's one game I'm definitely watching round at Dad's.

Wednesday 28th March
5.50 p.m.

Boys' night in at Dad's flat. England v Albania.

In attendance:

Dad, pining for Mum.

Bobby, pining for Emma.

Yours truly, not pining at all. But for the nagging doubt about Edinburgh I'd be feeling really smug right now. Compared to this pair of losers I'm quite the ladies' man.

'It isn't over, you know,' says Bobby, the moment Dad goes out to check on the chilli.

It's about the only thing he can cook. Chilli con carne and baked potato. He's on another of his *Men's Health* diets. No change in the waistline, but he produces lots of gas.

'What isn't over?' I ask, as if I didn't know. Emma's cheating heart is the only thing Bobby talks about. He doesn't even come out with useless facts any more. He's too *depressed*. I feel like telling him that it's a bit rich with his track record, but he is my mate.

'Emma and this lad. She's been seeing him again.'

'How do you know?'

'I called for her last night but she was out. When I asked where she was her mum got all flustered.'

'Wouldn't really stand up in court, would it?' I ask.

'She's seeing him, all right. You just know when somebody's messing you around. You get vibes.'

This vibe-getting might come in useful after Edinburgh. I

mean, I know Julie wouldn't, but I need to know, just in case she did . . .

which she wouldn't . . .

. . . would she?

I want to ask Bobby about it but Dad comes in with our tea. It'll have to wait.

Wednesday 28th March
10.00 p.m.

I arrive home dead on time. Mum lets me stay out until ten o'clock on a weekday, half past ten or sometimes even eleven at the weekend.

The moment I walk through the door I can feel that something is different. I wonder if this is what Bobby means by vibes.

'That you Terry?'

I do my usual.

'No, it's the Pope.'

'How was the match?'

'England won 3–1. It was OK, that's about all.'

Just then Mum giggles, and not at my match report. She sounds all high-pitched and girly. So what's going on? I reach the living-room door and there's this man.

He's a six-footer; short, blond hair; smart casual clothes. They're sitting on the couch side by side. Mum looks flustered and her hair's dishevelled. Oh gross, she's been snogging Marathon Man right here in our living-room!

'Terry,' she says, the aftershock of the giggle still rippling through her. 'This is Richard.'

Richard stands up and holds out his hand for me to shake. I give him the cold fish treatment. He's shaking hands with a mackerel.

'Nice to meet you, Terry.'

I say nothing.

'Typical teenager,' says Mum, desperate to end the uncomfortable silence. 'They just stop talking. Why is that?'

Richard doesn't seem to know because he just stands there with this wrinkled grin on his face. 'It's getting late,' he says.

Mum accompanies him to the door. By the time she's

finished saying goodnight, I'm already in my room listening to CDs through my earphones. Mum takes the hint and leaves me to it.

Friday 30th March
11.00 p.m.

I walk through the door high on the smell of Julie's hair, the dab of perfume on her throat. We hung around the bowling alley most of the evening. Sure, it meant having to be polite to sour-faced Kelly and to Fitz and his mates, but my reward for putting up with the Scouse mafia was a kiss and a cuddle at the bus stop. With Julie that is, not the Scouse mafia. Actually, Fitz walked past while we were kissing. I'd give my right arm for a photograph of the look on his face.

'Ignore him,' Julie told me. 'He's only jealous.'

I smiled. All sorts of things were going on behind the scenes tonight. Fitz and I nearly came to blows at one point when he wouldn't stop ribbing me over United. Then Paul and Pepsey had this big row and Pepsey stormed off home. There at the bus stop I didn't care. I was with Julie and that's what counted. When we're together like we were tonight, when I smell her hair and taste her lips, I can't believe that anything will ever come between us. I don't just think, *I know*, that we're for keeps. Then, the moment I'm on my own again, shadows start to form in the backwoods of my mind. Shadows of Frisky Fitzy. Shadows of blue-faced Bravehearts. I know I'm probably being paranoid, but nothing I do can hold back the shadows. Then I'm scared, really scared, that Julie's out of my league. I think and I think, and the more I think the more I convince myself that I'm just a skinny nerd that no girl in her right mind would be seen dead with. Once I'm in this mood there's always something there to remind me of the bad times. The times when Julie and Fitz were together.

Tonight the trigger for the shadows is tomorrow's game at Anfield. The last time we played Liverpool we lost 1–0 and Sky Sports showed Fitz with his arms round Julie, smirking into the camera. It was the worst day of my life. It was like he'd stuck his hands into my heart and flipped it inside out. What's to stop it happening again, I wonder? They'll be part of the same gang going to the match. What if it brings back old memories? The next two weekends are vital. The two biggest tests for our relationship so far: Anfield then Edinburgh. They could set the seal on a dream come true or they could bring everything crashing down.

Saturday 31st March
12 noon

High noon. Liverpool v United at Anfield. Liverpool haven't done the double over us since 1979, but they look up for it today. They do a team huddle under the heavy, perpendicular rain. I feel nervous. We've only played well once since Christmas. It's as if running away with the Premiership title has taken the edge off our game. It isn't just the match, either. I'm still thinking about Julie and Fitz. That game at Old Trafford. The 1–0 defeat. The sight of Fitz hugging Julie right there on the TV screen. It was almost more than I could bear. And they're together again today. There's a gang of them at the match: Gary and Kelly, Paul and Pepsey, Julie and Fitz. While Dad makes the sandwiches and Bobby drones on about Emma and how she's hurting him so badly I concentrate on the crowd, as if I'm going to be able to pick them out from a crowd of nearly fifty thousand people.

Both sides come close in the first five minutes, Robbie Fowler for Liverpool, Dwight Yorke for United. In the next five minutes honours are still pretty even, a chance for Liverpool through Sami Hyppia, one for United through Wes Brown.

'Come on, lads,' says Dad. 'I don't want to be eating humble pie at work this time as well.'

That's when it all goes wrong. After sixteen minutes Barthez makes a poor clearance and Gerrard hits a wonder strike from thirty yards.

One nil to Liverpool.

Dad slumps in his armchair. I crane forward to try to get a glimpse of Julie in the heaving crowd. If Fitz dares . . . No, I tell myself, don't let yourself down. I won't be jealous. I won't be conquered by the green-eyed monster. It's over between them. She's with me now. There's nothing to be jealous of.

After the first goal Liverpool have us on the rack.

'They've got you on the rack,' says Bobby, as if reading my mind.

Dad tells him to shut up. I lob a Coke can at him. He shuts up.

Then, forty minutes in, Fowler takes a Gerrard cross superbly and scores. Two–nil to Liverpool.

'Game over,' says Bobby.

Dad tells him to shut up. I lob the Coke can at him again. This time he doesn't shut up.

After sixty-six minutes something finally goes our way. The best move of the match is finished off by Dwight Yorke. Dad and I rise from our seats.

'Yes, 2–1. Here comes the fightback.'

That's when Bobby tells us the linesman has given offside. I throw the Coke can at him for the third time.

'What's that for?' Bobby complains. 'It wasn't me. It was the linesman.'

'I couldn't reach the linesman,' I explain.

Half an hour later it's gloom and doom here in Dad's living-room. Liverpool have become only the third team to do the double over us since the Premiership began.

'You'll have to play better than that against Bayern Munich,' says Bobby.

Dad and I scowl at him, but we both know he's right. We're getting a bad feeling about the game.

Saturday 31st March
11.15 p.m.

Special dispensation. Mum's letting me stay out till midnight. Julie knows this club called *Scene One*. It holds under-eighteen nights once a month. There's no booze allowed on the premises for these events. The management make a big deal about that to reassure parents. All it really does is make sure most kids stay well away. Still, I get to be with Julie, so who cares? Julie's dad is picking us up at 11.45 p.m. Mind you, I would feel better about being here if Mum wasn't having Richard round. Marathon Man's starting to get his feet under the table. The idea of that creep trying it on with Mum makes my blood boil.

The scoreline at Anfield has also taken a bit of a shine off tonight. I mean, it's great dancing with Julie, but I'm getting loads of grief off Kelly, Gary, Paul and Fitz over the result. Julie, Pepsey and Kelly clatter away to the loo leaving us lads hanging round like spare parts.

'What was the score?' slurs Fitz.

'Have you been drinking?' I ask.

Fitz bursts out laughing.

'What do you think? Everybody's at it.'

Everybody except me, it seems.

'We've got a stash of alco-pops hidden in the corner,' Fitz boasts.

'You'll get yourselves thrown out,' I say.

'So what was the score?' asks Fitz, ignoring me.

He's nothing if not repetitive.

'Quiet tonight, aren't you?' asks Fitz.

'Leave it, eh?' I say. 'You're getting boring.'

That just sets Fitz and his mates off again.

'Two nil, two nil, two nil, two nil . . .'

'OK,' I say, trying to stay cool. 'I get the message.'

'Two nil, TWO NIL!'

'Look,' I say, 'knock it off, Fitz.'

He pulls me to one side.

'I'll knock it off,' he snarls. 'When you give me my woman back.'

'*Your* woman?' I say. 'Julie made her own mind up, Fitz. You're pathetic.'

I turn away. The mocking laughter goes between my shoulder blades like a knife. Then my ear starts to burn. Fitz has hit me. I snap round and land him one on the side of the face. Worse the wear for drink, he staggers back and crashes on to the dance floor. I look up. With immaculate timing, Julie has just come out of the toilets.

Oh, wonderful!

There's a bit of an argument with the bouncers.

Have we been drinking? Cue innocent faces all round.

Perish the thought!

It's touch and go, but Julie and Kelly finally persuade them not to chuck us out.

Saturday 31st March
11.50 p.m.

We're waiting outside for Julie's dad. I phone Mum. She'll go ape if I'm late. Plus, there's another good reason for making the call. Julie's not too happy with me for hitting Fitz. I'm giving her time to calm down. It doesn't work. The moment I finish the call, she's down my ear.

'I thought you had more sense,' she says. 'Fighting in the club.'

'He hit me first!' I protest.

'That's what you always say.'

That's out of order. Fancy bringing up the evening I broke Fitz's ankle.

'Listen Julie,' I say, taking her hands. 'It was true then and it's true now. It's Fitz, he always starts it.'

Before she can answer, Julie's dad arrives and we get in. Pointedly, Julie climbs in the front and I'm left to twiddle my thumbs in the back. We sit quietly all the way home. I hardly get a goodnight, never mind a kiss.

God, I feel miserable.

Sunday 1st April
11.30 a.m.

I phone her at home. She's gone out with Kelly.

Sunday 1st April
11.45 a.m.

I phone her on her mobile. It's switched off.

Sunday 1st April
1.30 p.m.

I phone her at home. There's no-one in.

Sunday 1st April
6.00 p.m.

I've been phoning all afternoon. It just rings out. Not this time. Somebody's picking up. At last! It's Gerard.

'Julie, it's the Mad Manc.' Then the inevitable: 'Hey, what was the score?'

Julie takes the phone.

'Yuh?'

Her voice is cold. It doesn't sound like her at all.

'Are you angry with me?'

'Nah.'

'Sure?'

'Nah.'

'No, you're not angry, or no, you're not sure?'

No answer.

'Can I see you tonight?'

'I'm revising.'

'Am I in the dog-house?' I ask.

Julie sighs: 'I told you, I'm revising.'

'I'll see you tomorrow in school, then.'

'Yes,' she says. 'Tomorrow.'

I'm in the dog-house, all right. Woof sodding woof.

Monday 2nd April
8.30 p.m.

It wasn't easy, but I persuaded her to come round to mine. Mum's out jogging with Tricky Dicky the Marathon Man, so we're baby-sitting Amy. Amy's on the phone to Katie, so I drag Julie into the living-room.

'Look,' I say, 'I shouldn't have hit Fitz but he did hit me first.'

Julie rolls her eyes.

'You're as bad as each other.'

'No,' I say. 'No, we're not. If you only knew what he was like, what he's really like.'

'Terry, I should know. I went out with him for six months.'

'Yes, but . . .'

'And he never showed an ounce of aggression.'

140

'Yes, but . . .'

'And he's the one who ended up in plaster, not you.'

'Yes, but . . .'

'Yes, but *what*?' she asks.

That stumps me. Finally I manage a feeble:

'Yes, but I really like you.'

Oh, terrific! Could I be more lame? I could have at least managed the three little words.

Julie smiles. Joy! She's smiled. I'm forgiven! Pat me on the head. Tickle my tummy. I'll sit up. I'll beg. Just don't put me back in the dog house.

'Am I forgiven?'

She hugs me.

'Of course you are, but I wish you weren't so paranoid over Fitz. It's you I'm with. Forget him.'

'Forget who?' I ask, palms outstretched.

Julie laughs.

'Seriously,' she says. 'Don't put me under pressure, Terry. There's nothing between me and Fitz any more.'

I nod.

'I know.'

'So no more third degrees?' she asks.

'No.'

'And no more fighting?'

'No.'

'And you're not going to worry about him any more?'

I say no.

I think . . .

. . . maybe.

Tuesday 3rd April
9.10 a.m.

The Manc-baiting is starting to get me down.

I was edgy enough already, what with United playing Bayern tomorrow and Julie going away on Friday. But the defeat at Anfield has ripped my insides out. I've just walked to school in a thunderstorm. I'm soaked to the skin. I could really have done with my Nanook of the North coat. As a result of the downpour I arrive completely sodden and sit through registra-

141

tion with my teeth gritted. I'm steaming. Steaming with the central heating drying my clothes. Steaming with the humiliation of defeat. Then Six Guns drives the final nail in the coffin. He hands out a letter. It's the final deadline for the return of coursework. Stapled to it is a timetable for the GCSE exams. Until now I've been living in a fantasy world. If I don't acknowledge the exams, they can't happen. But they are happening, and too soon for comfort.

'Everything OK?' asks Julie when we meet in the corridor.

I give a lopsided smile.

'Is it the exams?' she asks.

'Yes.' (Among other things.)

'You can still get a C in Maths, you know.'

Sure, and Michael Owen will sign for Man U.

'Anything else bothering you?'

'No,' I say, lying through my teeth, 'just the exams.'

'Here,' she says, pulling me to one side.

She gives a quick glance left and right and plants a smacker on my lips.

'Better?'

The warmth of her floods through me.

'Mm,' I murmur.

'Demons all gone?'

'Definitely,' I say, as convincingly as I can.

But the demons never go far. They just hover over the horizon planning their next attack. Gone, you might say, but not forgotten.

Tuesday 3rd April
9.35 p.m.

United, returning the love. Ha!

Not any more. United 0, Bayern Munich 1. Me and Dad gutted. Bobby respectfully silent. I stare into space. I can't believe it.

Tuesday 3rd April
10.20 p.m.

I watch the ten o'clock news, just to make sure it's happened. It has. I watch Sergio's eighty-sixth minute winner go in, first at full speed and then in slow motion. I stare at the screen, numb with disbelief.

Wednesday 4th April
8.45 a.m.

I stand in the pouring rain outside the newsagents. I've been reading the back page headlines. Maybe if I pinch myself I'll find out it's all a dream. It isn't. It's a nightmare. I read the same headline over and over again:

United 0 Bayern 1. It's Becks to the wall.

I still can't believe it. We've got to win in Munich's Olympic stadium by more than two goals. It isn't impossible, but it isn't far off.

Julie comes up behind me and puts her arms round my waist. She rubs her chin against my back. As sympathetically as any Scouser could.

'Upset, aren't you?'

My reply is a kind of moan rising from my stomach. Eventually I manage:

'I can't believe it.'

Wednesday 4th April
5.30 p.m.

But it's true. We're on our way out of Europe. Bayern just don't give a lead away at home, not in twenty years of football. United's European dream is disintegrating before my eyes. I was hardly involved in the school match tonight, a 2–2 draw with St Leo's. I got subbed at half-time. Now I'm sitting in the changing room amongst the sweat haze and the steam and the piles of muddy kit. Fitz and co are taking the Michael something chronic.

Losing it? they ask.

Lost the plot? they ask.

United on the wane? they ask.

And all I can do is sit and take it. Half the reason for existing, my being a Red, seems to be disintegrating right in front of my eyes. I couldn't stand it if the same happened to Julie. Edinburgh is in two days. I'm dreading it.

7

I watch the coach pull away. Julie waves goodbye. I trudge through the rain. What a week. United lose in Europe. Leeds and Arsenal both win while Liverpool draw against Barcelona at the Nou Camp. *The rest show United how it's done*, one of the papers said. Are we losing it? Is it the end of our era of domination? It's hard to take. Through everything that's happened: Julie going out with Fitz, my parents' divorce, struggling at school, I've had one thing going for me. I was part of the Red Tribe, a United fan, a supporter of the greatest club in the world. It set me apart. I was somebody. I can't go back to the way it was when I was little, living in the shadow of Liverpool. Bobby's waiting for me on the corner. Funny how things turn out. It used to be me who hung round playing gooseberry. Now he's the saddo.

'She's gone then,' he says.

'Yes.'

'Don't look so miserable,' he tells me. 'She's back Sunday, isn't she?'

I nod.

'But?' asks Bobby.

'Well, I don't like the idea of Fitz being up there with her.'

Bobby goes into this big lecture. Love's about trust, he says. Jealousy will drive her away, he says. She's crazy about you, he says. Somehow I can't take advice from him right now. It isn't long since he was stringing two girls along and hankering after another.

'So how's your love life?' I ask.

'Ouch,' says Bobby. 'Low blow.'

144

'Sorry,' I say.

Just to make me feel even worse he says:

'Look, I know I'm not in any position to give advice but you've got something special with Julie. I'm jealous. Honest. So are all the other lads. Don't do anything to mess it up, Terry. Take it from somebody who knows.'

All of a sudden, I'm seeing Bobby in a different light. I'm reminded of that old movie Mum watches over and over again on cable. Yes, we're in Casablanca after the girl's flight has taken off. I'm Rick and Bobby's the short French guy.

'Bobby,' I say. 'This could be the start of a beautiful friendship.'

He thumps me on the arm and we kick and trip each other all the way up the road.

Saturday 7th April
9.00 p.m.

'Terry,' Mum calls. 'Julie's on the phone.'

I fly downstairs and pant Hello into the mouthpiece. She's talking through a tunnel of sound.

'Where are you?' I ask.

'Edinburgh.'

'Yes, I know that. Where in Edinburgh?'

'The disco.'

She sounds like she's having fun. There's a lot of noise in the background. Male noise.

'Who's that?'

'Oh, just Ian and Billy.'

Ian and Billy? Who the hell are Ian and Billy?

'Say hello lads.'

Ian and Billy shout down the phone. They're speaking Scottish. Either that, or they've got a mouthful of gravel. Come on, Julie, the last thing I want to do is talk to a couple of blue-faced Bravehearts.

'Will you do me a favour?' Julie asks.

'What's that?'

'I'll be on the way home on the coach when the FA Cup semi-final is on. Phone me on my mobile when the goals go in.'

145

'OK.'

'Got to go now,' says Julie.

Go! But you haven't said anything.

'Julie . . .'

Too late, the line's gone dead. I stand staring at the receiver. I've been waiting all day for a call and what do I end up doing? I talk to a couple of mad Scotsmen and promise to tell her the Liverpool score. Not the world's most romantic phone call.

Sunday 8th April
3.30 p.m.

Bobby and I exchange miseries all the way to Dad's.

For him, it's Emma and her cheating heart. Plus a dog that uses his room as a toilet. Lady's latest crime – eating the fascia of his mobile.

It's the phone I'm moping about too, Julie's phone call from hell. (Well, Scotland.)

Either way, neither of us feels much like smiling. When we arrive at Dad's, R. Kelly is belting out: *Turn back the hands of time*.

'Should I turn it down, lads?' he asks.

'No.' I say, 'Up.'

Sunday 8th April
5.00 p.m.

Things are looking up. Wycombe are holding Liverpool. Could a giant-killing be in the offing?

I hope so.

Sunday 8th April
5.30 p.m.

My mobile goes. Julie.

'I thought you were going to phone me when the goals go in,' she says.

'I am. It's still 0–0.'

'But they're half-way through the second period.'

'Sorry, but it's true. And Wycombe should have had a penalty.'

'Call me when something happens.'

'You can count on me.'

Sunday 8th April
5.33 p.m.

Something's happened. I phone Julie.

'Yes.'

'1–0 to Liverpool. Heskey.'

Julie relays the news. The coach erupts. A clenched fist of noise. I hear Fitz's voice above the others. Guess what he's yelling?

'What's the score, Manchester?'

Sunday 8th April
5.38 p.m.

More news.

'Julie, it's 2–0 to Liverpool. Fowler.'

Again she relays the news. Again the coach erupts. Yes, and again Fitz puts in his two-pennyworth.

Sunday 8th April
5.43 p.m.

More news.

'Julie, it's 2–1. Wycombe have got one back.'

Stony silence on the coach. A wall of sound in Dad's living-room.

Sunday 8th April
5.50 p.m.

Full-time. Liverpool have won.

'This time,' Bobby whispers as I punch in her number. 'Say the three little words. It's easy.'

'But you've always told me the opposite,' I remind him.

'That was then,' says Bobby, 'this is now. Say them, the three little words.'

'Easy for you,' I shoot back. 'You've never meant it.'

'Low blow number two,' says Bobby. 'I meant it with Emma.'

I'm through to Julie.

'It's all over. Liverpool v Arsenal in the FA Cup Final.'

The coach erupts. Bobby mouths the three little words and digs me in the ribs.

'Thanks Terry,' says Julie. 'I can't wait to see you.'

Bobby opens his eyes so wide they could pop out.

THREE LITTLE WORDS, YOU MORON.

But the three words I come up with are these: 'Yes, me too.'

D'oh!

Sunday 8th April
7.00 p.m.

Bobby's in the loo so I have a go at sorting things with Dad.

'You OK?'

'Yes, can't grumble.'

'You know what I mean.'

'You mean, have I got over shooting myself in the head?'

'Something like that.'

Dad gives a wry smile.

'Some things you don't get over, Terry. Your mum's the best thing that's ever happened to me, and I've given her up on a whim. You know what I am? A pillock is what I am!'

Which is about as close as Dad will ever get to opening his heart. By the time Bobby is off the loo and we're down the stairs and in the street, we can hear Harry Nilsson blasting out of the upstairs window: *Can't live if living is without you.*

'Sounds like he's picking up,' says Bobby. I kick him on the ankle.

Sunday 8th April
10.30 p.m.

Bobby's gone and Amy's in bed so I have a go at sorting things with Mum.

'You're serious about this Richard fellow, aren't you?'

'He's a lovely man.'

'And Dad?'

'He's a lovely man who dumped me. Or did you forget that little detail?'

'So there's no way back?'

'No Terry, it's final. I thought my marriage was for keeps. I know my divorce is.'

Monday 9th April
4.30 p.m.

We're at the swimming pool. A new kind of baby-sitting duty. We picked up Amy and Katie and came straight here after school. Amy and Katie are messing about at the shallow end, and we're at the deep end. So it's just Julie and me. No Sabrina lookalike friend trying to shoot me down in flames. No Scouse mafia taking the Michael. Just the two of us. Julie dives in. She looks sleek and gorgeous in a black Speedo costume. She's the only girl who makes my throat go dry every time I look at her. She surfaces next to me and gives me a hug. I glance at the lifeguard but he's not looking.

'I can't wait for the holiday,' says Julie. 'Then we can do this all the time.'

'Two days left,' I say.

Edinburgh indeed! As if I had anything to worry about.

Tuesday 10th April.
12.00 noon

I've got something to worry about. And how!

I just overheard Fitz talking to Gary. The conversation went something like this:

Gary: How was Edinburgh?

Fitz: Special.

Gary: Yes? How come? Did you score? Spill the details, maestro.

Fitz: Well, I don't want to boast.

Gary: Boast all you like. You don't get a reputation like yours for nothing. That's why they call you Frisky Fitzy.

I know exactly why they call him Frisky Fitzy. I try to hear more. No good. Their voices are lowered to a whisper. I hear the odd *never* and *you dirty dog*, but I can't make out anything else. Which is why I'm standing here outside the canteen with my guts kicked out. But Julie, you wouldn't do this to me. You couldn't.

**Tuesday 10th April
3.30 p.m.**

Could you?

**Tuesday 10th April
8.00 p.m.**

Julie, no.

**Tuesday 10th April
10.00 p.m.**

NO!

**Tuesday 10th April
Midnight**

NO-O-O-O-O!!

**Wednesday 11th April
12.15 p.m.**

'What's with you?' asks Bobby. 'You look like a zombie.'
  'I hardly slept.'
  'How come?'
  I tell him what Fitz said to Gary.
  Bobby just laughs: 'Never.'
  'They went out for six months, didn't they?'
  Bobby makes a big deal of thinking about it then repeats:
  'Never. Not in a million years. I've seen you together. You're made for each other.'
  'Bobby, I heard him boasting to Gary.'
  'Did you hear Julie's name? Well, did you?'
  I shake my head.
  'Not in so many words.'

150

'Then give the girl a chance, you moron. Who do you trust, Julie or Fitz?'

'Julie, of course.'

Only I say it with a lump the size of a duck's egg in my throat.

'Look, if Fitz has been messing with anybody, it isn't Julie. There were eighteen other girls up in Scotland. It's got to be somebody with a track record, somebody who's done that sort of thing before . . .'

His eyes widen like he knows something.

'Give me some time and I'll get to the bottom of it.'

'You?'

Bobby winks.

'Yes, me. You've got something good going on, Terry Payne, and I'm not going to let you and that green-eyed monster on your shoulder mess it up. You'll let me do this for you, won't you?'

I nod. Cue Bobby as the Seventh Cavalry.

'And you won't go asking Julie any of your stupid questions?'

I shake my head.

'Promise?'

'I promise, OK, even if I have to chew my own tongue off.'

'Feeling better?' he asks.

I shrug for his benefit, but the answer's no, not really.

Wednesday 11th April
3.15 p.m.

End of term for everybody but the football team. We're playing Stonebridge in the Cup semi-final at four. Julie gives me a cheery peck on the cheek and sets off to pick Amy up.

'See you later,' she calls.

'Yes, see you later.'

I watch her go and I just can't believe she'd mess around with Fitz. Not after everything she's said. I mean, it's been just about perfect. Nothing could spoil what we have. But I heard what I heard. I pick up my football kit and head for the changing rooms. Football? The way I feel right now I couldn't even manage Subbuteo.

Wednesday 11th April
3.45 p.m.

I'm sitting on the steps outside the changing rooms watching the rest of the team drifting across the field. I catch a glimpse of Bobby. He's doing the business all right. Sherlock Holmes has got nothing on him. He's talking to Pepsey. Why's she still hanging round? They look animated. What gives?

Wednesday 11th April
3.47 p.m.

Now he's talking to Paul. Huh?

Wednesday 11th April
3.50 p.m.

Now Emma. But she should be long gone, too. I mean, it *is* half-term.
   What *is* going on?

Wednesday 11th April
3.55 p.m.

I'm lacing up my boots when Fitz waltzes in. I look away. I don't even want to look at him.
   'Heard the team selection?' he says, 'you're out and I'm in.'
   I sit, brooding. I could kill him. But I promised Bobby I'd keep a lid on it.
   'You're a loser Payne, always have been . . .'
   Anger's climbing up inside me, like mercury in a thermometer.
   '. . . always will be.'
   Sorry Bobby, but that does it. I'm on my feet. In my mind's eye I'm already shoving my fist in his face, yelling; *This is for Edinburgh*. I don't even get the chance. Just as I'm about to cross the changing room floor, Paul bursts in and lands a right-hander smack on Fitz's nose. No warning. He just pops him one. And this is one of Fitz's best mates! Gary jumps up and restrains Paul.

152

'What's going on?' he asks.

Fitz is kneeling on the floor, blood streaming from his nose. It was a punch Lennox Lewis would have been proud of.

'Paul,' says Gary. 'What do you think you're doing? What's wrong?'

Paul is red in the face and struggling to get at Fitz.

'Ask that dirtbag.'

He shifts his attention to the dirtbag who is kneeling on the changing room floor. The dirtbag starts to rise groggily to his feet. Paul sticks out a foot and dumps him back on the tiles.

'You're supposed to be my mate, Fitz,' yells Paul. 'I know what happened in Edinburgh.'

What happened in Edinburgh! Of course, it wasn't Julie Fitz was talking about yesterday. It was *Pepsey*. Fitz is the one she's been seeing. He's the reason for all those panicky looks at the bowling alley.

Oh joy! Julie, how could I ever have doubted you? I'm a jealous skunk who ought to be put down. I'm a lousy rat not fit to kiss your feet. I'm a . . .

I'm still cursing myself for my jealousy when Bobby walks in. What's he doing in the changing rooms? He dropped out of the team months ago. I soon find out. Bobby marches over and elbows Paul out of the way.

'Get up, Fitz,' he says. 'It's my turn now.'

Your turn! Now what, Bobby?

Fitz is still trying to staunch the flow of blood. He holds up the flat of his hand in a gesture of abject surrender.

'You're going to get what's coming to you,' says Bobby, balling his fists angrily. 'Emma's told me everything.'

Emma!

Emma and Fitz!

Pepsey and Fitz!

He *has* been putting himself about.

But not Julie and Fitz.

The Prescot One is innocent!

Bobby's still trying to get Fitz to fight like a man when Six Guns marches in.

'What's the hold-up, lads? Stonebridge are already out on the pitch.'

That's when he sees Fitz.

153

'What the . . . ?'

Gary jumps in with an instantly-concocted cock and bull story.

'It's my fault, sir. I opened the locker and caught him in the face.'

Six Guns screws up his face. He isn't convinced by the cock or the bull. But he doesn't have time to go into it.

'Let's see that nose.'

He shakes his head.

'You're in no state to play, John lad. Terry, you're in midfield.'

Six Guns shouts to the other teacher who helps with the team.

'Mr McArdle. See to John, will you? It could even be broken.'

Fitz groans out loud. I look at Bobby and he winks.

'Play your heart out, Terry.'

Wednesday 11th April
5.15 p.m.

As it happens, I did play my heart out. We won 3–1. I set up the third goal for Paul. He was playing like a man possessed. It's like he saw Fitz's face on every player he tackled. His performance ripped the heart out of Stonebridge.

I shower and change. I pump Bobby's hand and shower him with all the praise he can take.

He's a genius.

He's a star.

He's a . . . mate.

'That'll do me,' he says. 'Now knock it off. Go and tell Julie those three little words.'

I'm about to go when I think of something.

'What about Emma?'

'It's over. Still, there's plenty more fish in the sea.'

Fish. Sea. That's the old Bobby talking.

'So you weren't really in love?' I ask.

Bobby shrugs.

'I got kind of obsessed, I suppose.'

'Ah,' I say. 'Obsession.'

His mobile goes.

'Hello Mum. Yes, I stayed after school to watch Terry play. I'll be home in twenty minutes.'

He switches off then nudges me.

'Did you know the average teenager spends twenty per cent of their income on mobile phones?'

I smile. A fact, a genuine useless fact. Bobby's back all right.

I set off up the hill running like a lunatic. I've never felt so alive.

Three little words, just say those three little words.

Past the police station, three little words.

Past the library, three little words.

Past the Fusilier, three little words.

Wednesday 11th April
5.30 p.m.

Julie meets me at the front door. I grab her round the waist and swing her in the air.

'You're happy. Did you win?'

Oh, I won all right. Look at me, I'm on top of the world!

I tell her about the match, but first I tell her all about Fitz and Paul and Pepsey and Emma and Bobby. Her eyes go so wide you wouldn't believe.

'Fitz did? That two-timing . . .'

I place my finger on her lips before she can say another word.

'Julie, who cares about Fitz anyway? He's not even worth worrying about.'

That's a bit rich coming from me and Julie knows it. She gives me this long, hard look. It's like she's searching for the green-eyed monster. After a few moments she throws her arms round me and says: 'I love you, Terry Payne.'

'*You* love *me*! No, I'm supposed to say it. *I* love *you*.'

You dufus malufus, Payne. You've been practising all the way home and you forget to say it.

'That was my line,' I complain.

'But I said it first,' says Julie.

'And you really mean it?'

'I wouldn't say it if I didn't.'

'Did you ever say it to Fitz?' I ask.

Julie shakes her head disapprovingly.

'I thought he wasn't worth worrying about.'

I gulp big style. Oops, rumbled.

'He isn't,' I say. 'Now shut up and kiss me.'

She does. We're still kissing when Amy walks in. She gags and walks out again. But who cares? This is possibly the best day of my life.

Saturday 14th April
12.45 p.m.

I answer the front door. It's Julie. She's come straight to Dad's flat from gymnastics.

'Dad,' I say, leading her into the living-room. 'This is Julie.'

'Ah,' says Dad, with a twinkle in his eye. 'The *lovely* Julie. Terry's told me all about you.' Julie blushes.

'What's the score?' she asks, slipping off her jacket.

'2–2,' I tell her. 'Coventry are making a fight of it.'

'Leeds hammered your lot on Good Friday, didn't they?' says Dad.

I glare at him.

'Sorry,' says Dad. 'It's the Manc in me talking.'

'Don't worry,' says Julie. 'I get used to it with Terry. We've got to beat Everton on Monday.'

The second half starts. It's better from United. They're moving better, Keano driving them forward in droves. But Coventry are defending heroically.

Then, just when it looks like the Sky Blues will hang on for a draw, Ryan Giggs heads the breakthrough goal.

3–2 United.

Just to put the icing on the cake, Paul Scholes hits a twenty-five yarder.

4–2 United.

'You know what?' says Dad, 'if Arsenal lost at home to Middlesbrough today, we would be Champions.'

'Yes,' I say, 'like that's going to happen.'

Saturday 14th April
5.00 p.m.

It's happened!

We're at Liverpool Lime Street station, waiting for the Prescot train (Julie was shopping, I was hanging round looking bored) when we hear the news on the radio. Arsenal 0, Middlesbrough 3. I can't help it, my arms fly straight up in the air and I'm singing at the top of my voice:

'Championes, championes . . .'

Julie slaps her hand over my mouth, but the words come out all the same, echoing across the station forecourt.

'Ole, ole, ole.'

Julie's struggling to keep me under control.

'Terry, we're in the middle of Liverpool.'

But I don't care. United, champions again. Returning the love. Same as Julie. I grab her round the waist and swing her round and round.

'I know, but we're champions. Three titles, back to back.'

Julie smiles and drags me on to the train.

'Will you shut up?' she says looking round.

'But I'm happy,' I tell her.

'Ever heard of quiet-happy?' she asks.

'No,' I say.

Wednesday 18th April
7.49 p.m.

'That's it,' says Dad, head in his hands, 'it's all over.'

Me, Dad, Bobby and Julie are clustered around the television for United's must-win showdown with Bayern Munich. 1–0 down from the first leg, we've got to win 2–0 in Munich. Fat chance of that now. Giovanni Elber has just stolen in between Jaap Stam and Wes Brown and swept the ball into the roof of the net. Just four minutes into the game it's 1–0 to Bayern. 2–0 on aggregate. Disaster.

'You're right there,' says Bobby.

I don't even have the energy to throw a drinks can at him. We had an Alp to climb, now it's a Himalaya.

157

After seven minutes they hit the crossbar. The idiot commentator says it's good for United!

Yes, like bacon's good for pigs.

We get some good chances ourselves but nothing quite goes right, and five minutes before the break Scholl puts Bayern 2–0 up, 3–0 on aggregate. Even Bobby's silent. Julie squeezes my hand.

Wednesday 18th April
8.49 p.m.

'Y-eeeee-sssss!!'

Ryan Giggs opens the second half by lobbing Kahn.

We're 2–1 down. Is it possible? Could we get two goals back? Is the spirit of Barcelona still alive?

Wednesday 18th April
9.45 p.m.

The answer is no. We've been outmanoeuvred home and away. Bayern deserved to beat us.

'Gutted?' asks Julie as we walk up the street with Bobby in tow.

'Yes,' I tell her, 'and then some.'

'You don't know what gutted is,' scoffs Bobby. 'My team's just lost to her lot in the Merseyside derby.'

Julie winks.

'And we're going to keep on beating you, Bobby.'

Bobby shrugs. Like all good Evertonians he's learned to take the rough with the smooth.

'Probably,' he says.

We reach the street corner. I go to turn right. Julie and Bobby turn left.

'Hey, where are you two going?' I ask.

'Bobby's got a new girlfriend,' says Julie mysteriously. 'Don't you want to meet her?'

I frown.

'Do you know who it is?'

Julie grins.

'Oh yes.'

'So who . . . ?'

My question is answered by the appearance of Kelly Magee at the other end of the street.

'Not Sabrina, the teenage Scouser!' I exclaim.

'Got it in one,' says Bobby.

'But she's already got a boyfriend. What about Gary?'

'What about Gary?' asks Kelly. 'He started slagging off one of my mates so I dumped him.'

'I don't . . .'

'Pepsey,' explains Kelly. 'Paul and Gary started calling her all sorts of names for what happened up in Edinburgh. They blame her even more than Fitz. I asked Gary why a lad who goes out with two girls is a stud, but a girl who goes out with two lads is a slapper. Gary said I was talking rubbish. I gave him the elbow. I'd been getting fed up of him anyway.'

'Oh yes,' says Julie, 'and Kelly's got something to say to you, Terry.'

'Yes?'

Kelly pulls a face, like she's got something really hard to say.

'I was wrong about Fitz, and about you. I stuck up for the wrong one. Sorry.'

Sorry! Miss Superscouse has just apologised. To the Mad Manc!

Wednesday 18th April
10.00 p.m.

I'm at the bus stop with Julie, waiting for her bus. We've just left Bobby and Kelly.

'Bit of a turn up for the book, that,' I say.

Julie shrugs her shoulders.

'One thing I don't understand,' I say.

'What's that?'

'You and Kelly sticking up for Pepsey. Don't you think what she did was a bit off?'

'Of course I do, but lads get away with it all the time. She doesn't deserve the sort of treatment Paul and Gary have been giving her. They've both done the same.'

'Have they?'

'Of course,' says Julie. 'Don't you keep up with the gossip?'

I shake my head.

Julie laughs and kisses me.

'You know what you asked me the other day?' she says. 'Whether I ever said the three little words to Fitz?'

I nod my head, my heart hammering.

'Well, I didn't. I've never said it to anyone but you. You're the only one, Terry, the only one.'

I hug her until my arms ache. Her bus pulls up and she starts to climb on board. There's only one thing to say:

'I love you, Julie Carter.'

8

What a difference a few months make. I still remember Sunday, 17th December, a day that will live on in infamy. Liverpool won 1–0 at Old Trafford that day and I had to endure the sight of Fitz simultaneously hugging Julie, *my* Julie, and celebrating Danny Murphy's winner. I hated Sky Sports for that, zooming in on that sleaze pawing the girl of my dreams. I suffered agonies during the Littlewoods Cup Final and when Julie went to Edinburgh. Fitz was there both times and I feared a repeat of Old Trafford. Everything has changed now. Julie is back in Cardiff for the FA Cup Final and I know I've nothing to worry about. Sure, Fitz is down there too, but they are *so* finished. After what he did with Emma and Pepsey, Julie thinks he's the biggest slimeball on Merseyside. Not everything changes for the better, of course. Over the last month, Mum has been seeing more and more of this Richard character. He's all right, I suppose. He's serious about Mum. He's quite funny, in an old-fashioned Jasper Carrott sort of way, and he doesn't try to take over. Yes, he's all right, but only as a casual acquaintance. But something tells me this acquaintance is anything but casual.

'Weird, isn't it?' says Dad, interrupting my thoughts. 'This time two years ago it was us closing in on the Treble. Now it's Liverpool.'

It's true. We're champions again, but since we got knocked out of Europe the end of the season has been an anti-climax. Now all we can do is watch Liverpool chase their dream of the Littlewoods Cup, FA Cup and UEFA Cup. One down, two to go. What makes it even weirder is: how do I feel about it? Do I go with my instincts and will disaster on our enemies from the other end of the M62, or do I support them for Julie's sake? Dad has no doubts:

'Liverpool against Arsenal?' he grunts. 'Pity one of them has to win.'

I smile. That's the classic Man U point of view, of course. A plague on both their houses.

It's a beautiful sunny day here in Prescot and down in Cardiff. There are seventy-two thousand people in the Millennium Stadium for the first FA Cup Final held outside England. It's all Arsenal in the first half and Liverpool ride their luck in the seventeenth minute when Henchoz handles Thierry Henry's shot in the penalty area.

'Jammy beggars,' says Dad.

Julie will be having kittens.

In the last twenty minutes of the first half Arsenal stoke up the pressure. It's total domination.

When the half-time whistle goes, Dad gives his verdict:

'The Scousers are going to do it, you know. The Gunners aren't taking their chances. Classic pattern, weather the storm then hit them with a sucker punch.'

Julie agrees. She phones me on her mobile from Cardiff.

'We've come through the worst,' she says. 'Watch us turn it on in the second half.'

I scan the crowd for a gorgeous girl on a mobile. No sign. The second half follows the pattern of the first and in the seventy-second minute Ljundberg scores for Arsenal. Suddenly I know which side I'm on.

'Yiss!' I cry.

Then, in the eighty-third minute Michael Owen volleys home the equaliser. I slump back in my chair.

'Told you,' says Dad. 'It's Liverpool's year.'

After that Arsenal are rocking. In the eighty-ninth minute Owen scores his second, Liverpool's winner, his shot sneaking inside the far post. The moment the final whistle goes, Julie is back on the phone.

'I've got three people who want to talk to you,' she says.

It's Gerard, Josh and John-Joe. They're singing at the top of their voices:

'Are you watching, are you watching, are you watching Manchester? Are you watching, Manchester?'

I hold the phone to Dad's ear.

Now they're singing: *Who led the Reds out? Hou, Houllier!* Dad pretends to puke. The TV cameras zoom in on a Liverpool banner reading: *What we can achieve in life echoes in eternity*. The moment I read it, I know that's exactly right. Maybe I can do something Mum and Dad didn't manage.

'Julie,' I shout against the maelstrom of sound around her, 'I want us to be forever.'

'What?'

'You and me forever.'

'Yes, of course.'

I can't say how happy that answer makes me. The massed ranks of Liverpool fans take up the Kop anthem: 'You'll never walk alone.' OK, I know they're the enemy, but it's a song that makes the hairs on the back of my neck stand up. Suddenly, there she is, wearing the gold Liverpool away shirt. She's got her scarf raised aloft. Every hair I've got is standing to attention. I see Fitz two rows back. He's looking at her and realising what he's missing. That's when Julie's dad spots the TV camera and points it out to Julie. She gives this heart-stopping smile and mouths the magic words:

'Love you, Terry.'

There won't be another Sky Sports viewer who understands her words, but I do and that's all that matters. We will be forever.

Wednesday 16th May
7.30 p.m.

For the UEFA Cup Final I'm wedged uncomfortably between Gerard and Julie on a two-seater settee. Josh, John-Joe and Julie's mum and dad are shoe-horned into the three-seater. All eyes are glued to the wide-screen TV.

'We could do with a good start,' says Julie.

Scrub that. It's a *dream* start. Markus Babbel heads the first goal after just four minutes. I'm immediately engulfed in roaring boys and cushions. As the match progresses the Liverpool fans boo Alaves midfielder Jordi Cruyff every time he touches the ball. He committed the crime of once playing for United! After sixteen minutes the Scouse elation is more than

I can bear. Gerrard has just struck home a Michael Owen pass.

'Easy, easy,' chant Gerard, Josh and John-Joe.

Julie snuggles up happily.

But after twenty-six minutes it becomes obvious Alaves are not just in Dortmund to make up the numbers. Their substitute Ivan heads one back for the Spanish side. I allow myself a quiet smile. But as Alaves allow chance after chance to go begging I resign myself to a Liverpool win. It gets even worse on after thirty-nine minutes when McAllister converts a penalty. More cushions, more roaring boys.

I phone Dad at half-time.

'Are you watching?' I ask.

'Yes, unfortunately.'

Three minutes after half-time Moreno heads into the Liverpool net at the back post. 3–2. A comeback? Surely not. But two minutes later it is 3–3. Moreno again. It's stunned silence in the Carter household. They all look at me.

'What?'

With less than twenty minutes left, Robbie Fowler scores.

'That's the winner,' says Mr Carter authoritatively.

More boos for Jordi Cruyff. The Scousers are enjoying themselves. They don't enjoy the eighty-eighth minute. Cruyff scores an amazing equaliser. 4–4. Yes, United bite back! All around the room heads are in hands, fingernails are between teeth. Julie's stopped snuggling. But Liverpool are too strong in extra time. A tiring Alaves have two men sent off and hand Liverpool the cup with a headed own goal.

'It's a good job we won,' says Julie. 'Or you'd be going home without a goodnight kiss.'

She's joking, of course.

Isn't she?

Saturday 19th May
3.45 p.m.

It's the boys' club again. Julie and Kelly have taken a day off gymnastics to go to the Valley for Liverpool's final game of the season so Dad, Bobby and I are eating crisp butties, swigging Coke and watching the match on TV. It's 0–0.

'I hope Charlton realise they have my future happiness in their hands,' says Bobby, the die-hard Evertonian. 'I couldn't stand it if Liverpool got the quadruple. I mean: three cups and qualification for the Champions' League, that's just greedy!'

'How on earth are Liverpool still level?' Dad complains. 'They could easily be two or three down. They're going to do it, you watch, hang on for dear life then score a late winner.'

'Don't burst a blood vessel,' says Bobby. 'A Dutch survey has shown that male heart attacks rise by fifty per cent during football matches.'

Dad and I glance at Bobby. He's back to his old self. As it turns out, Liverpool don't snatch one late winner, they get four. Fowler scores two, Murphy one and Owen one. At the same time civil war has broken out at Old Trafford. It looks like the United board are trying to force Alex Ferguson out. After all he's done for us! I can feel Liverpool breathing down our necks.

'We're never going to hear the end of this,' groans Dad.

I'm certainly not. Julie rings at full-time to rub it in. In the nicest possible way of course, but she's still gloating. She's especially delighted at our end to the season. We've lost 3–1 at Spurs.

'Three defeats in a row,' she says, 'that's the sort of Treble you don't want.'

'We've already sewn up the Championship,' I remind her glumly. 'Nothing to play for when you've walked it by some distance.'

'It's the last time though,' says Julie. 'No easy ride next year. The Kop-ites are back.'

'We're still number one,' I say stubbornly.

'Not for long,' chuckles Julie. 'Next year we're going to win the Premiership and the Champions' League.'

'I think Fergie might have something to say about that,' I retort.

'If he's still at Old Trafford,' says Julie.

The banter carries on for a few moments before she smoothes my feathers with a whispered:

'Love you lots.'

I answer likewise and ring off.

'Do you think it can last?' Dad asks dubiously.

'Of course,' I say.

Sunday 20th May
3.00 p.m.

And it's true. Julie and me are going to last. If you've got any doubts, then listen to this. Do you know where I am today? Queen's Drive, Liverpool. That's right, I've joined the Carter family to see Liverpool bring their trophies back home. There are four hundred and ninety-nine thousand, nine hundred and ninety-nine Liverpool fans on the streets and one Manc, **me**. I'm keeping pretty quiet about my football affiliations but, honestly, isn't that the greatest sacrifice you can make? Greater love hath no man than to applaud Liverpool for the one he loves?

After half an hour waiting under Rice Lane flyover, the team buses pull into view. Elated voices boom around the concrete structure as the players raise the three trophies aloft. My mind goes back two years to the May evening when Dad and I joined thousands of others to welcome Man U home after their Treble. Is this it? Is the balance of forces shifting back to Merseyside? That's all I hear as we walk back to the Carter family car, a plush, new people-carrier.

'A tale of two Trebles, eh?' says Mr Carter, reading my mind.

'Our time will come again,' I say.

'Without Ferguson?' says Julie. 'I don't think so.'

Sunday 20th May
Sunset

After the parade, we played footy in Croxteth Park, had a meal in a pub in Crosby, then set off for the beach. Now the sun is setting over Crosby marina and Julie and I are strolling along the sand in our bare feet. The rest of her family are packing up ready to go.

'That's a big sun,' I say, looking out towards the wind farm.

'Yes,' says Julie, 'a *beautiful* big sun.'

'Do you think we will make it?' I ask, 'you know, think we can be forever?'

'I don't see why not,' says Julie. 'But you never know what tomorrow will bring. Maybe it's better just to enjoy today.'

I mull this over for a few moments.

'No,' I say, 'forever's better. That's what they get in the movies, happy ever after and a walk into the sunset.'

'We've got the sunset,' says Julie. 'Do you want to walk into it?'

I squeeze her hand tightly.

'Don't mind if I do.'

Also by Alan Gibbons

Julie and Me . . . and Michael Owen Makes Three

It's been a year of own goals for Terry.

- Man U, the entire focus of his life (what else is there?) lose to arch-enemies Liverpool
- he looks like Chris Evans, no pecs
- Mum and Dad split up (just another statistic)
- he falls seriously in love with drop dead gorgeous Julie. It's bad enough watching Frisky Fitzy (school golden boy) drool all over her, but worse still she's an ardent Liverpool FC supporter.

Life as Terry knows it is about to change in this hilariously funny, sometimes sad, utterly readable modern Romeo and Juliet story.

THE LEGENDEER TRILOGY
The Shadow of the Minotaur

'Real life' or the death defying adventures of the Greek myths, with their heroes and monsters, daring deeds and narrow escapes – which would you choose?

For Phoenix it's easy. He hates his new home and the new school where he is bullied. He's embarrassed by his computer geek dad. But when he logs on to the Legendeer, the game his dad is working on, he can be a hero. He is Theseus fighting the terrifying Minotaur, or Perseus battling with snake-haired Medusa.

The trouble is The Legendeer is more than just a game. Play it if you dare.

Vampyr Legion

What if there are real worlds where our nightmares live and wait for us?

Phoenix has found one and it's alive. Armies of blood-sucking vampyrs and terrifying werewolves, the creatures of our darkest dreams, are poised to invade our world.

But Phoenix has encountered the creator of *Vampyr Legion*, the evil Gamesmaster, before and knows that this deadly computer game is for real – he must win or never come back.

Warriors of the Raven

The game opens up the gateway between our world and the world of the myths.

The Gamesmaster almost has our world at his mercy. Twice before fourteen-year-old Phoenix has battled against him in *Shadow of the Minotaur* and *Vampyr Legion*, but *Warriors of the Raven* is the game at its most complex and deadly level. This time, Phoenix enters the arena for the final conflict, set in the world of Norse myth. Join Phoenix in Asgard to fight Loki, the Mischief-maker, the terrifying Valkyries, dragons and fire demons – and hope for victory. Our future depends on him.